———————— ★ ————————

Again a scurry in the woods. Had one of the dogs gotten loose? As Nolan turned, fire exploded in her eyes. She felt herself falling back, back into the black water. Something immovable landed on her, holding her down. She refused to breathe—wondering if the water would ruin the Armani evening pants and the Japanese tunic that was worth over five thousand dollars.

Still no chance for breath.

I can't die, I have to write the check for the caterer. She tried to push back but her fingers clawed at something slippery, hard, unyielding. The dark of the sky and the dark of the water moved closer, closer. She knew better: she refused to breathe. Until she couldn't refuse any longer.

———————— ★ ————————

Previously published Worldwide Mystery title by
VICTORIA HOUSTON

DEAD MADONNA

DEAD HOT SHOT

Victoria Houston

WORLDWIDE®

TORONTO • NEW YORK • LONDON
AMSTERDAM • PARIS • SYDNEY • HAMBURG
STOCKHOLM • ATHENS • TOKYO • MILAN
MADRID • WARSAW • BUDAPEST • AUCKLAND

For the minnows:
Madeleine, Harry, Margaret,
Violet, Louisa and Lincoln

Recycling programs
for this product may
not exist in your area.

DEAD HOT SHOT

A Worldwide Mystery/August 2009

First published by Bleak House Books.

ISBN-13: 978-0-373-26682-1

Printed in U.S.A.

What if you suddenly saw that the
silver of water was brighter
than the silver of money?
—Mary Oliver
"How Would You Live Then?"
Blue Iris

ONE

NOLAN REECE STUMBLED down the flagstone stairs only to stop midway. One hand on the wood railing, the other holding her wineglass high, she wobbled in place, hoping she hadn't spilled all the wine. High up over her left shoulder an owl hooted. She jerked around, eyes searching, but black clouds streaking overhead shut out the moon. No wonder she couldn't see.

Should've skipped the champagne, you silly, she thought. Wine sloshed across her right foot, soaking the toe of one of the velvet slippers that had cost four hundred goddamn dollars—but what the hell, this was her night. The owl hooted again—the great horned owl that she had glimpsed only once in her forty-two years of running up and down these stairs. Nolan made a mental note to try to remember to ask her secretary to find out how long owls live. Could it be the same one she saw when she was twelve?

Swaying against the railing, she turned to look up and back toward the top of the stairs. Lights shone from every window in the big house, casement windows custom designed to replicate the tall, narrow lines of the majestic pines that swept up and up and up. Even the panes held patterns: pine needles etched into the glass.

God, what it had cost to keep those trees, to force the architects to find a way to nestle the house into the hill without cutting a single one of her trees. Worth every penny and every hour of argument. Hell, it was the beauty of the house hidden among the trees that first caught the eye of the writer from Architectural Digest. That and the amazing circumferences of the logs she'd had shipped down from Canada. Well…also the soft silver glow of the wood that had required twenty-six coats of stain before she was happy. And Andy had fought her on every decision. What was he thinking? It wasn't even his money.

Though the November air was cold and crisp, the windows facing west were half open, letting the heat of the party—laughter, voices pitched high in friendly argument, a caterer's clatter of pots and glassware— flow towards her. Nolan took a sip from her wineglass, then held it high: a toast to the people behind the windows. It had been a perfect party.

Well, almost perfect. Blue had arrived an hour late. An hour late for her own engagement party? That was more than a little selfish of her. If the guests hadn't all arrived and needed Nolan's attention…well, she'd deal with Blue in the morning. All she had to do was remind her: in my house you follow my rules or I change the terms of your trust and you see no money until you turn forty. An empty threat, true, but Blue didn't know that.

What was the girl up to anyway? First she had insisted on staying in the guesthouse instead of her own lovely suite in the big house. Nolan herself had chosen the fabrics, the furniture, the antique doll collection—oh, those priceless dolls from the Civil War era! Then, when Nolan had called on the intercom to hurry her down because Barry and his parents had arrived, there was no answer. Not even Barry knew where she was.

I'll get to the bottom of this. Nolan set her jaw as she turned towards the lake. If Blue is so stupid as to be fooling around with that boy from up the road again... She took a sip of wine then started down the stairs. She'd bet anything that was it. She'd sure as hell put a stop to that just as she had managed to so far. Uncanny how those two gravitated to each other. And Blue tried to say they were just friends. Oh, sure—as if she was dumb enough to believe that.

Foolish Blue. Here's Barry, the perfect guy for her to marry: Dartmouth, Harvard Business School, an athlete, good-looking, a family business that could pay for her extravagances. His parents are so dear. Nolan herself couldn't have picked a better man for her daughter. Another sip of wine. And, of course, she had. Picked Barry for Blue that is. Years ago.

The kids were still at Country Day when Nolan got the idea. Right before she'd had to send Blue away. And then last Christmas, five years later, the two had run into each other at a party and—thanks to a little prodding from her and Miriam—they seem to have been together ever since. She had to admit she was surprised at how it all fell into place so easily. Until tonight.

Another wave of laughter from above and Nolan turned away, determined to resolve the issue of Blue's late arrival in the morning. Aside from that, the rest of the evening had gone precisely as Nolan had planned: the food was excellent and the new caterers quite competent, the two college boys tending bar were absolutely darling, and even Andy managed to be more sociable than usual.

Frances and Josie seemed to do okay. Their new clothes helped, of course, and Nolan had made sure they were introduced around. When the girls had skittered down to the media room to play pool and horse around, that had been fine. She had planned for that, too.

Reaching the glossy, dark green platform that fronted the long boat dock, Nolan heard a scurrying in the brush off to her right. She paused to listen. A crackle of leaves and sticks. A deer? A bobcat? More likely that muskrat that had carved its den in the roots of the big red pine beside the dock. A bear had been spotted on their peninsula—but a bear would make more noise, wouldn't it?

She stepped up and onto the dock, walked out over the black water, lifted her head high and ordered the universe to clear the clouds from the Milky Way.

"Now make a wish and kiss the moon goodnight," her grandmother had said so many years ago, rocking Nolan in her lap on this very dock. It was that memory of an uncomplicated time that bound Nolan to a daily ritual she missed only if she was traveling, if there was lightning, or if the wind chill hit below minus twenty. It was Grandmother's way of promising that life would never hold too many surprises: you can always kiss the moon goodnight. Not even Andy and Blue rolling their eyes on the overcast or rainy, snowy nights could keep her from that sacred moment. Always the wine, always the wish. Always the comfort.

WINEGLASS CLUTCHED in her right hand, she searched for the moon but could see only a shadow behind black, rushing clouds. Nor was the lake able to gather enough light for a reflection—the surface so dark she could hear rather than see the water.

A clinking off to her left. Nolan glanced across the dock. Damn! Jake left the bassboat in the water again. How many times did she have to tell that idiot to take five more minutes, press a button and raise it into the shore station? All right, if a storm blows in and damages the boat or the dock, he can pay for it out of his salary. Serve him right, the dumbyak.

Again a scurry in the woods. Had one of the dogs gotten loose? As Nolan turned, fire exploded in her eyes. She felt herself falling back, back into the black water. Something immovable landed on her, holding her down. She refused to breathe—wondering if the water would ruin the Armani evening pants and the Japanese tunic that was worth over five thousand dollars.

Still no chance for breath.

I can't die, I have to write the check for the caterer. She tried to push back but her fingers clawed at something slippery, hard, unyielding. The dark of the sky and the dark of the water moved closer, closer. She knew better: she refused to breathe. Until she couldn't refuse any longer.

"Mom looked pretty tipsy to me," said Blue as she stood with her fiancé and her father in the doorway after waving goodnight to the last of the guests.

"It's not the first time she's left a dinner party and just gone to bed," said Andy. "You know your mother." He was relieved that he'd managed to find Nolan's purse with the house checkbook so he could pay the caterers and the bartenders. Nolan wouldn't be happy about that. Now he knew how much she had spent on this affair and he was appalled. Thank goodness her father wasn't alive to witness her spending.

When the last guest had departed and Blue and Barry were on their way up to the guesthouse, Andy poured himself a glass of milk, selected one of the left-over dessert pastries that appeared to have cost twenty dollars each, let the dogs out one last time, then walked slowly up the stairs.

At the door to Nolan's bedroom, he paused. Balancing the pastry and the glass in one hand, he gave the doorknob a slow, silent turn and nudged the door open a crack. The room was dark. He listened. Quiet. She wasn't snoring. He knew better than to wake her—that could only lead to thirty minutes of harangue for something he probably did wrong tonight. Oh, well, deal with it in the morning, he thought, and pulled the door closed.

At eight a.m. the next day, a crisp, clear Thanksgiving morning, Andy followed the two golden retrievers down to the dock. Nolan was waiting. Though Loon Lake has dark water, it's quite shallow. Only three feet deep where his wife lay slumbering beneath gentle waves— arms still reaching for the sky.

TWO

HOPING TO SHUT out the shrill voices coming from his kitchen, Paul Osborne closed the bedroom door and resumed searching, for the second time, every pocket in his hunting vest. Then back to his brush pants—front pockets, back pockets. No luck. He re-checked the pockets in the Filson oilcloth that he wore on rainy days. Not even a forgotten cartridge. Looking around the room he exhaled hard, puffing his cheeks in exasperation.

Okay, he decided, I know it's absurd but... Yanking his fly fishing vest out of the closet, he tackled the Velcro on every one of its two million pockets: the horizontals, the verticals, the squares, the oblongs, the tubes, even the deep, wide, zippered pouches stuffed with fly boxes. Nothing was out of place.

He laid the vest on the bed and opened both the right and the left sides to expose the flat plackets sewn to the interior lining. With the vest on, these were spaces only a contortionist could reach. But who knows? Perhaps, in a moment of dementia, he had stuck it there? He slipped fingers into each hidden pocket, hoping... Nope. The hunting license was not to be found. Phooey. This was one time when that license was more than just a license.

He sat down on the bed to think. For a day of celebration, this Thanksgiving was not off to a good start. Why had he ever agreed to let Fred Merrill and that annoying wife of his, Kathleen, stay at his place until their new house was finished?

HE KNEW WHY: Kathleen had been so sweet and insistent that it would be "only two weeks" and "a wonderful favor that will save us at least thousand dollars." In retrospect he thought about that "thousand dollars." Baloney! Fred's a retired orthodontist. He has hundreds of thousands—for God's sake the man's got dollars up the wazoo! He should be spending, not saving.

Worse yet— that was five weeks ago. Five excruciating weeks spent with two people who weren't happy unless they were bickering, badgering and otherwise upsetting each other. Listening to Kathleen zing her husband with one snide remark after another until Fred would snap back reminded Osborne of life under the critical eye of his late wife—a memory that arrived with the old, familiar, chest-tightening chill.

What he couldn't abide was the contempt in their voices: it hit him right in the gut. He had never known exactly when it was that Mary Lee had stopped loving him—but she did, turning her into a woman with a tongue as unkind as Kathleen's. But Mary Lee was dead, she didn't live here anymore and the house was his. His alone, his sanctuary. At least it was before the Merrills arrived.

OSBORNE JIGGLED OPEN the top drawer of the lamp table beside his bed, knowing even as he did it was a fruitless effort. And it was. Still no sign of the flimsy computer printout tucked into its beat-up little orange plastic case, an innocuous item that was growing more precious by the moment. This wasn't just a trek to hunt grouse that he was after. That hunting license was his ticket to freedom—hours in which to ponder how he could boot the Merrills from his guest bedroom without appearing rude.

Then it occurred to him. Of course! Mildred's Food Shop never closed. He'd just stop by and get a duplicate. Cost him ten bucks but, hell, a small price to pay for peace and quiet. Now why hadn't he thought of that sooner?

MINUTES LATER, BACKING his car out of the drive, he was so eager to put the Merrills behind him that he pretended not to see Fred barge out the back door waving, pretended not to notice Mike going crazy in the back seat of the car—barking, tail wagging, throwing anxious looks back at his master. Had he forced himself to pay attention to the man waving so frantically, he would have seen the phone in Fred's hand. But he didn't, and so he drove to Mildred's Food Shop in peace.

Osborne rolled his window down and inhaled the fresh autumn air. The day was crisp and cool but sunny. The morning's frustrations slipped away, replaced with a light heart and a burst of energy. No problem planning the day now: he would hunt for an hour or two in the sunshine, giving Mike lots of exercise, then drive straight to his daughter's house for his first turkey of the day.

After that, home to change fast (during the hour he knew Fred and Kathleen were planning to dine at the Loon Lake Pub) and on to his second Thanksgiving with the one person with whom he would share his house, if she would only say yes. And if that Thanksgiving went really well…he might just stay over and avoid the Merrills all together—while having a very, very nice time. He made a mental note to pack his Dopp kit and a toothbrush just in case.

Osborne was still grinning as he pulled into the alley that ran alongside Mildred Taggert's ancient gray box of a building. As he drove down toward the shop that was attached to the back of the old house, he was glad to see the Open sign scrawled on cardboard and stuck in a side window. Yep, Mildred's Food Shop was one of Loon Lake's few sure things: you count on her being open, on the milk being fresh, the cooler packed with night crawlers—and immediate access to a license for hunting or fishing. He parked in front of the old barn that Mildred used for storage.

Striding across the drive towards the shop entrance, Osborne tripped over a chunk of broken asphalt. He cautioned himself to slow down. While Mildred might believe in retail, she sure as hell didn't put much stock in repair. Kicking aside a shingle that had drifted off the roof to land on the stoop, he reached for the doorknob, worn down to bare metal and dangling. Thirty years he'd been coming by the shop and thirty years that damn doorknob had been dangling.

Bells over the screen door gave a loud jangle as he pushed it open to enter the small shop with its familiar, musty smell. The place wasn't more than three hundred square feet but Mildred crammed it full. Shelves sagged under cans of soup, pickles and olives, boxes of cereal, bags of rice (white and wild), marsh-mallows, potato flakes, slightly squished loaves of white bread, bags of hot dog and hamburger buns, boxes of donuts, Danish and coffee cake. Redemption for the forgetful.

The aisles between the shelves were so narrow only a small child dared squeeze down most of them. In the far left corner a frosted-up refrigerator case held milk, assorted juices, worms by the dozen and a couple cartons of eggs. Random stacks of soda six-packs were scattered throughout the shop, teetering one on top of the other and adding to the challenge of maneuvering the aisles.

Osborne might have retired from the practice of dentistry but he would never lose the instincts that had drawn him to his profession. His eyes, long attuned to discerning discrepancies in small places, could never overlook the perpetual layer of dust covering many of the shelved goods. Streaks left by eager, reaching fingers only emphasized what was either Mildred's carelessness or her worsening eyesight.

Whatever the reason, the dust cast a gloom over the shop and, as always, caused him a frisson of worry: Did enough people come by? Was Mildred making enough to live on? Could she care for those girls? It was the well-being of the girls that really worried him.

But in the next instant, he would assure himself everything was okay. The shop was the same as it had been the last time he was there—and no bad news had surfaced since then. After all, Mildred had an instinct for what people were likely to run out of when the Loon Lake Market and the local gas stations were closed. He knew for a fact that he was hardly the only Loon Lake resident willing to risk death under a toppling shelf on a national holiday. Given that she opened at five a.m. and stayed open 'til ten, the cigarette trade alone was sure to keep her in business.

THE FINANCES OF Mildred's Food Shop were a favorite topic of Osborne and his buddies as they nursed their early morning coffees at McDonald's. "Yep," Pete Ratliff, the retired accountant among them would say, "if you start with minimal overhead for upkeep and add to that the free labor she gets from those foster kids of hers, plus her location and the increase in Loon Lake property values over the decades... Hell, old Mildred must be worth at least a million." Thoughtful heads would nod as someone echoed Pete's words, "Yep, at least a million."

ALWAYS AS THEY talked, Osborne would think about the girls. They were sisters off the Ojibwa reservation whom Mildred had taken in as foster children four years earlier. Frances Dark Sky, the oldest, was so shy that when she came for her annual dental exam, just to look at Osborne had seemed to cause her pain. Josie, younger than her sister by two years, was the polar opposite— ebullient, chatty, not in the least intimidated by an adult.

Osborne knew it was his own Métis heritage that

piqued his interest in the girls. Though he was not as nut-brown as they, his complexion was darker than most Loon Lake residents, the majority of whom were descended from a mix of northern European settlers. But even though the girls were full-blooded and he was only a sixteenth Ojibwa, his eyes were as black-brown and his forehead as high and wide as theirs.

The girls, of course, had no idea that he kept an eye on them, that he checked with the young dentist who had taken over his practice to be sure Mildred didn't skip their six-month cleanings and check-ups. And she didn't. The old woman might be crabby but she appeared to take good care of the girls. It helped that Osborne arranged for the dental visits to be free. Mildred was led to believe that the state paid.

"Seems the only thing old Mildred spends money on are those damn raccoons," Pete would add to his assessment of Mildred's net worth. Again the heads would nod in agreement: yep, you couldn't get in or out of Mildred's Food Shop without confronting a raccoon.

Granted they were dolls—stuffed animals dressed in outfits ranging from firemen to Peter Pan to ballerinas—but they were a bit overwhelming. Dozens crowded an overhead row of shelving that circled the interior of the store. Twins dressed in waders, red checked shirts and fishing hats, each holding a cane pole with a tiny plastic fish swinging from it, sat in a birchbark boat that hung over the cash register. A baby raccoon in diapers, a bottle of milk in one hand and a rattle in the other, snuggled up against the computer that printed the licenses for fishing, hunting and the harvesting of wild rice.

Osborne found the raccoons unsettling and he once made the mistake of commenting to his daughter, Erin, that Mildred's "thing for 'coons" caused him to question her mental state. "Oh, right, Dad," Erin had said. "And what about all the guys you know who hang dead deer—heads and shoulders—over their dining room tables, their living room fireplaces, over their beds for God's sake. At least Mildred's raccoons aren't dead. You know, she's had some of those dolls for years. They could be worth a lot of money."

"Well…" said Osborne, "I still think it's weird."

THREE

HE-L-L-O-O," SAID Osborne, raising his voice as he ambled towards the front counter. The interior of the shop had a way of reminding him of the shadows cast by ancient hemlocks: all sun was blocked out. Mildred saved on electricity, too.

Though the store appeared empty, he was well aware that the old woman was, as always when there were no customers, hunkered down in a beat-up armchair in a sitting room off to the right—one eye on a small portable television set, the other watching the shop through a half-open door. Sure enough, he heard the rustle of fabric. Then the door squeaked back and Mildred shuffled into the room, pushing her bulk into the tight space behind the counter. She wore a shapeless black shift that fell almost to the floor, skimming the top of scuffed black oxfords and exposing thick ankles encased in beige orthopedic stockings.

"Yeah, whatcha need?" Her voice was low, gruff. In all the years that Osborne had been coming by for a license or some groceries, not once had he seen Mildred smile or heard her greet him by name. Nor did she appear to change, not even with age.

MILDRED TAGGERT'S HEAD was remarkably large, large even for the imposing monolith of her body. Her face was doughy and puckered where dimples might have been (though Osborne found that hard to imagine). She had a nose that crumpled up and back and was too small for the width of her face. As if words were an extravagance, her lips were thin lines that barely moved when she spoke. Small, round, black lenses hid her eyes, lenses so dark he wondered how she could see anything in the dimly lit shop.

But Mildred's hair made up for the homeliness of her face and figure. Streaked in shades of black, white and gray, it had a wondrous sheen that reminded Osborne of the silk thread used on bamboo fly rods. The old woman herself seemed pleased with that hint of beauty: she let her hair flow back from her face in waves, then twisted it into a soft bun, which she anchored with an ebony spike.

OSBORNE WAITED FOR Mildred to position herself behind the counter. He knew what to expect as the script rarely changed. First that growl of "Whatcha need?" His answer to which was followed by the pointing of an arthritic finger in the direction of the requested item. Next a grunted "That's all?" And she rang up your purchase. If the request was for a license, she was just as succinct: "Name. Address. Birth date. Social Security." If someone balked at giving their Social Security number to an old woman they didn't know, her answer was blunt: "No Social, no license."

"Good morning, Mildred," said Osborne, determined to shake an extra word or two out of her today. "Gorgeous morning for a Thanksgiving, don't you think?"

"Whatcha need?"

"Well, I appear to have lost my hunting license and was hoping you could fix me up with a duplicate."

Before she could grunt an answer, they heard a loud crash in the far corner of the shop. "Whaddya do this time, Frances?" said Mildred, scowling as she leaned across the counter to look down the aisle.

The brown, burnished face of the young Indian girl showed itself above a stack of boxes near the refrigerator at the back of the store. Her eyes were wide and worried as she mumbled, "I just…I didn't mean to… this box fell."

"I know that—question is whaddya break?" Osborne didn't like Mildred's tone.

"Um, I'm checking—maybe salad dressing? But I'll get it cleaned up, Ms. Taggert."

Osborne watched as Frances scurried to pick up several jars and bottles that had rolled along the floor. She glanced up suddenly and caught him staring at her. She looked away fast as if expecting him to bark at her, too.

"Frances," said Osborne, his voice gentle, "what do you think of our new dentist—the one who took over my practice?"

"She sees 'im just like the state says she has to," said Mildred.

"Thank you, Mildred, but I was talking to Frances," said Osborne, without taking his eyes off the girl. She had grown since he'd last seen her. Her face was fuller with an angular beauty of its own: remarkable cheek-bones, a square jaw and a wide, generous mouth that drooped to the left when she smiled. If she smiled. Osborne could never help thinking poor Frances, poor Josie—those poor girls... The only time he ever saw the sisters was when they were working in the shop—never outdoors, never with friends their own age. And he knew Mildred could not be easy to live with.

Before Frances could answer Osborne's question, Mildred was demanding: "Name? Address? Birth date? Social Security? Ten bucks." With a sigh that implied he knew she knew his name, Osborne provided the information.

"Where's Frances going to school next year?" he said as he opened his wallet to reach for a bill. "She'll be in college, right?"

"Ask her," said Mildred with a dismissive jab of her thumb. But when Osborne looked back down the aisle, the girl was gone. She had vanished behind the curtained French doors that led to the living areas of the old house.

DECIDING TO LET Mike out of the car before he left, he put the dog on a leash and guided him along the alley and past the storage barn to a vacant lot. God forbid Mike poop in Mildred's yard. Not that it mattered—Mildred's passion for raccoons included a live one, which she kept in a wire cage at the front of the barn. Attached to the cage was a white sign painted with yellow flowers and the name "Daisy." The cage was elevated so the animal's droppings littered the ground beneath it.

In Osborne's eyes, Mildred's affection for her pet redeemed her crabbiness: somewhere under all that black fabric and behind the dark glasses, the woman must have a heart. He just hoped that that miniscule evidence of warmth extended to the Dark Sky sisters.

But this morning, as Osborne neared the cage, he was surprised to see that the cage door was slightly ajar and Daisy nowhere in sight. He stopped, holding the leash tight. Raccoons are canny—quite capable of jimmying the kind of latch used on the cage. Canny and confrontational. The last thing he needed was for Mike to tangle with an angry raccoon.

Looking up, he checked to be sure the animal hadn't found its way onto a branch of the old oak that hung over the fence from the house next door. He peered up at the barn, wondering if the critter might be inside. No sign of the raccoon, but the barn was interesting. Contrary to expectations, Mildred appeared to have put some money into the place: new windows gleamed in the sunlight. Casement windows in new frames no less. Expensive.

Of course, the outer walls hadn't been touched— the mustard yellow paint still peeling and dusty with age—and the door leading into the barn was battered as always, though it sported a shiny brass padlock. But the door was closed so Osborne hoped that Daisy was either inside or long gone.

Keeping an eye out for trouble, he held Mike on the leash until they had walked past the barn and were standing on the edge of the vacant lot, a field of tall grass toasted golden brown by early frosts. A quick scan showed no movement so he unleashed the dog. Mike trotted off sniffing eagerly. He gave a quick spin and set about his business.

"Here, Mike," called Osborne when the dog was done. But a sudden breeze enchanted the air-scenting lab, pulling him towards something hidden in the grass. Nose down, he snuffled, lingering even after Osborne called again.

"You goofball," said Osborne, walking over to check out Mike's prize. He was expecting a dead rabbit and hoping like hell the dog wouldn't roll in it. It was a carcass all right, but one too fresh for rolling. A raccoon wearing a collar ringed with yellow plastic daisies lay on her side, dead. And judging from the fresh blood pooling under her body, Daisy had not been dead long. Out of curiosity, Osborne nudged at the blood-soaked fur near her left ear. She had been shot and not with a BB gun—a bullet from a .22 caliber pistol maybe?

Osborne sat back on his heels. He was certain Mildred wouldn't have done this to her pet. So who did? What mean-spirited person would harm a little critter like Daisy?

More disturbing was that someone had fired a gun within the city limits—a highly illegal act. Out of town you can shoot as many gophers and prairie dogs as you wish—but not in midtown Loon Lake. He'd definitely mention this to Lew when he got to her house later. A dead animal wouldn't be serious enough to ruin her Thanksgiving dinner but as the Loon Lake Chief of Police, she needed to know that someone was firing a weapon too close to homes and schools.

Getting to his feet, he wondered if he should tell Mildred. Or should he hope that she would assume that Daisy ran off—and never know the truth?

A scream shattered the sunny silence of the vacant lot. Osborne looked back towards the barn and the shop. If he had been in the woods, he would have thought it was the cry of a rabbit losing its head to an owl. But he wasn't in the woods. That was a human scream. But of anger? Pain? Terror? Leashing Mike, he ran back towards the shop.

FOUR

THE SHOP WAS EMPTY. Silent. "Mildred?" Osborne called out. No answer. "Mildred!" He raised his voice. Still no answer. Threading his way past cereal boxes and jars of condiments, he managed to get to the end of one narrow aisle without a disaster. He rapped on the French doors leading to the living room of the old house. "H-e-l-l-o-o? Mildred?"

From somewhere beyond the doors, he could hear voices rising and falling. A fevered discussion was taking place in a distant room. "You old biddy—you can't make me!" A girl's voice, followed by the sound of a slap. No wonder they couldn't hear him.

He was about to rap again when he heard Mildred say, "Josie! So long as you live here you do as I say and I told you I don't want to see that bum around here again. I'll call the cops on the son-of-a-bitch. You hear me?"

Osborne certainly heard her. Sounded to him like Mildred had enough on her hands. Forget the raccoon. He backed away from the French doors and hurried down the aisle doing his best to make as little noise as possible. At the entrance to the shop, he held the dangling doorknob until the door had closed without slamming.

THIRTY MINUTES LATER he was trudging down a gravel road that led to the logging lane he had promised Mike. The land, which belonged to the paper mill, was open to hunters and had long been Osborne's favorite spot for hunting birds: grouse, a few pheasant that escaped from a nearby preserve, a random woodcock.

Setting out on a hunt had a way of reminding him of a time in his late teens when he had considered becoming a sculptor—until his father gave him a short course on the reality of the artist's life vs. the financial guarantees of dentistry. He hadn't regretted following in his father's footsteps. Not only did he enjoy the profession and discover that he was very good at it, but dentistry held an unexpected benefit: it sharpened his eye for volume, line, color and shape. As a result, a successful hunt could yield more than an entrée for the dinner table—though he didn't see that at first.

He was in his forties before he realized it wasn't the game he was after so much as the hunt itself. Hunting forced him to watch for the slightest movement in the forest cover, to listen for the faintest whisper. Hunting drew him close to the heartbeat of the forest and it was that that he loved.

That and the unexpected. Walking through woods where the only paths were those made by deer, he often stumbled onto totems of past lives—animal, vegetable, even mineral—that haunted the northwoods.

He saw skeletons of ancient trees whose immense, rotted caverns seemed hushed with secrets; bones of animals delicate and detailed in the patterns left as they fell; carcasses of cars burned and abandoned by owners Osborne guessed to be mobsters from Chicago anxious to hide evidence of bootlegging. He had yet to find a corpse in one of the burned out vehicles but he wouldn't be surprised when he did.

And the more he enjoyed a hunt—or an evening of fishing—the more he was likely to recall the badgering of his late wife: "Paul," Mary Lee had said too many times to count, "how much longer until we've got enough of a nest egg that we can move to Milwaukee? You know you'll have so many more patients there and make a lot more money…"

Somehow that nest egg never happened—not even when Mary Lee added separate bedrooms to her pouts and punishing silences. Again, he had no regrets. He might not be worth as much as Fred Merrill, but for over thirty years he had been able to hunt within minutes of his home—and fish off his own dock. A lifestyle money can't buy.

THE DOG BOUNDED AHEAD, sniffing here and there, levitating in sheer bliss. Under normal circumstances, Osborne would be sharing Mike's enthusiasm, but not today. He couldn't get his mind off the dead raccoon, off the anger in Mildred's voice, off that single, piercing scream.

What had the girl done that was so bad she deserved to be slapped—and slapped so hard he could hear it in the other room? Not like he hadn't had to discipline Mallory and Erin when they were in their teens—though he had never laid a hand on them. Grounding had worked.

Osborne tried to keep his mind in the moment as

he followed the lab down the rutted lane. He signaled the dog to find birds and Mike charged into a thicket of young aspen peppered with balsam. Osborne followed, running. But instead of listening for the flutter of a flushed bird, he thought again of poor dead Daisy. Maybe he should have said something? If he had, he might have been able to see for himself that the girls were okay…

A bird flushed, catching Osborne by surprise. Raising his shotgun, he pulled the trigger even as he knew he was too late. The bird was long gone. "All right now, get your act together," he said aloud to himself. "This is one of the last fine days of autumn. Pay attention."

The thicket gave way to a sea of black-brown cattails, their velvet cones split and ravaged by autumn winds. Mike ran along the edge of the swamp to where it bordered a hardwood forest of maple, oak and white birch. Just a few weeks earlier they had hunted here, but all was changed: the luminous reds and russets of the leaves had disappeared—vanquished by ever-hardening frosts. The trees were barren now, their black-brown branches thrust skyward as if to steel themselves against the harsh gusts of winter.

Again Mike flushed a bird and again Osborne shot too late. Mike didn't know—he wagged his tail in anticipation of the command to retrieve.

"Sorry, fella, but I think we better give it up," said Osborne. "I've got too much on my mind. I'm just not sure I did the right thing." Mike looked longingly in the direction the bird had flown, then turned quizzical eyes on his master. He tipped his head and waited.

"I know what you're thinking," said Osborne. "And you're absolutely right. We need to stop by Erin's for a second opinion."

His daughter's van was parked on the street in front of her house, the rear door open and only the seat of her tan corduroy slacks, the back of her black sweater and the tail of her long blond braid visible as she tugged at something inside. "Erin?" said Osborne from where he stood on the sidewalk.

"Dad!" The youngest of his two daughters backed out of the van and turned around, a smile of surprise crossed with consternation filling her face. "You're an hour early." She checked her watch. "The kids are still with Mark over at his folks' place. I just came home to check on the turkey and start the potatoes.

"Here, help me with this." She handed him a cardboard box with two pies inside, then reached back into the van for a baking dish covered with foil. With a kick of one foot, she slammed shut the door of the van. "We had brunch over there and now—"

"I'm not here for dinner," said Osborne, interrupting as she turned towards him. "I just…do you have a minute that I can run something by you? See if you think I did the right thing? And I'll be back later."

Erin paused to study his face. "You look worried, Dad. Is it serious? You didn't…did Lew break up with you?"

"Heavens, no."

"Okay, then. Come on in and we'll talk—but no need to leave and come back. You may as well stay now that you're here."

"Well, I won't do that, sweetheart. I plan to go home and change. I am not coming to your Thanksgiving dinner in hunting gear." He followed her up the stairs and onto the porch of the roomy, old Victorian home she shared with her husband and their three children. As Erin shoved the front door open with her shoulder, they were hit with a heavenly aroma.

"Smell that turkey, yum!" she said as they walked through the living room, past the dining room with its long table set for Thanksgiving dinner and into the kitchen where she set down the cardboard box and reached for an apron flung across the kitchen table. "So what's up, Dad? Hey, cup of coffee? I have to make some for later anyway."

"Sure." As the coffee brewed, he told her what he had found in the vacant lot, how he had heard a scream, and the frightened look on the face of Frances Dark Sky when she knocked over the box in the shop. "That was Mildred's pet raccoon," he said. "With that little daisy collar—it had to be."

"And you're sure it had been shot? Not chewed by some dog or… Or maybe—you know, Dad, there's been a bear getting into the garbage cans at McDonald's."

"Erin, I'm a deputy coroner, a dentist and a hunter. I may be retired from my dental practice but I sure as hell know a bullet wound from a dog bite."

"Yeah, you're right, you're right… " Erin leaned back against the kitchen counter, arms crossed as she mulled over his story. Osborne waited, hoping she would agree he'd done the right thing. "I don't know, Dad," she said after a long minute. "Mildred's such an irascible old soul—you hate to give her another reason to be cross."

"That's what I've been thinking. I don't want to be responsible for one of those girls being accused of something they didn't do."

"Of course, you don't know that they didn't do it," said Erin as she handed him a mug of hot coffee. "But whatever happened, it's Mildred's problem—I think it's wise you decided to mind your own business."

She gave him a fond look, then checked her watch again and reached to turn on the gas burner under a large pot filled with potatoes that had been peeled and cut into chunks. "How's the rest of your day going?"

"Oh, jeez, don't even ask," said Osborne, rolling his eyes. "I am a desperate man, kiddo."

"Kathleen and Fred at it again?"

Osborne nodded as he sipped his coffee. "Never ends."

"Speaking of the Merrills, I saw Kathleen in her car last week and—I know this is unkind, Dad, so just between us—have you noticed how much that woman resembles a pug? That square, pudgy face, and her lips are this wide, tight little line... " Erin held pinched fingers in front of her own mouth to demonstrate.

Osborne chuckled. "Poor woman."

"Not like she couldn't do something about it," said Erin, bending to open the oven door and check the turkey. "Drop a few pounds for starters. She spends enough money at the beauty parlor... " She whirled around from the stove. "Which reminds me, Dad, your ears should have been burning yesterday morning—burning." She gave him a teasing grin.

"Oh, no, what now?"

God, how he loved this girl, thought Osborne as they chatted. She was so different from both himself and his late wife. Erin had lucked out—inheriting the upbeat Irish genes from both sides of the family. Tall and slim with a complexion much fairer than his own, she juggled husband, children and pursuit of a law degree part-time—without losing her sense of humor or ever rushing a child or an adult who needed to talk.

"You've made quite an impression on your female houseguest, that's for sure."

"Really?" said Osborne with a twinge of dread.

"I had Beth and Mason in for haircuts at Jorene's Le Cuts yesterday and Kathleen was there. She was on her back in the shampoo chair with a towel over her face getting some sort of conditioning treatment so she didn't see us come in. And guess who happened to be the topic of conversation…" Erin spoke with a lilt that spelled trouble to Osborne.

"You're kidding, I hope."

"She was going on and on about you and Fred and your hair—"

"Our hair?" Osborne interrupted her. "Fred doesn't have any hair."

"Correct. Her exact words were, 'Then there's Dr. Osborne, same age as my husband, but he's got all his hair. Thick, black, wavy—silver at the temples. So-o-o good-looking in a man that age.'"

"Erin—you are exaggerating."

"Swear I'm not. And she went on. Said Fred's let himself get fat—but not you. She told the ladies in the

salon you've got the flattest stomach she's ever seen in
a man your age. You're sixty-three but you've got the
body of a fifty-year-old." Erin grinned at him. "I'm not
sure if that's a compliment, Dad."

Osborne put his head in his hands.

"And while old Fred sits around fussing with his fly
rods or watching the History Channel, you're always
on the go."

"I'm on the go, all right. Trying to keep out of the
line of fire between those two." Osborne stood up and
walked over to set his coffee mug in the dishwasher.
"That's it. I have got to get those people out of my
house. Tomorrow if I'm lucky. And you're not pulling
my leg? Kathleen really said all that stuff—in public?"

"D-a-a-d, she's got a crush on you."

He threw up his hands. "Let's call Mallory. I know
she's not planning to visit until Christmas but maybe I
can change her mind and she can catch a plane this
afternoon. I'll buy the ticket. Then I can tell the
Merrills they have to move out of her room."

"Forget that. She's on deadline for her thesis plus
she's invited to Thanksgiving dinner with the parents
of that guy she's been seeing. And you shouldn't have
to make excuses, Dad. It's your house. You simply say
that it's time for them to find somewhere else to stay
because you have plans."

"I do? What kind of plans?"

"Dad…" Erin looked at him in frustration. "That's
not the point. Whatever plans you have or don't have
is none of their business."

Just then the phone rang. Erin stepped around the

corner into the den where they kept the cordless phone and answering machine. "Whoa," she said as she reached for the phone, "we've got six messages! Hello?" As she listened, she walked back into the kitchen and handed the phone to Osborne. "It's for you. Lew has been trying to reach you all morning."

FIVE

"GOOD MORNING, Lewellyn. Happy Thanksgiving," said
Osborne, eager to hear the voice of the woman who
made his day every time she turned her sparkling dark
eyes his way.

"Doc, where the hell have you been? I've been calling all over for you. Don't you answer your cell phone?"

Ouch, maybe the eyes weren't sparkling. Snapping,
perhaps?

"Sorry, Lew. I was out for birds this morning so I
didn't think to take the phone."

THAT WASN'T EXACTLY the truth. Given that it had
been less than a year since Osborne had been able to
have his own landline—a standard home phone that
didn't have two elderly ladies listening in as he took
his calls on their shared party line—the cell phone
remained a novelty. And a novelty less than reliable:
not only does Loon Lake exist in the peripheral
vision of cell tower developers, but trees, hills and
wooded shorelines conspire to block the few cell sig-
nals available.

Just last month he and Lew had been heading west
towards a trout stream only to pass a woman standing

on the roof of her Toyota sedan. No need to stop and ask if she needed help—it was obvious she was trying to get a cell phone signal.

But this was no time to make excuses.

"WHAT'S UP?" SAID Osborne, hoping the eagerness in his voice would atone for the frustration he'd caused.

"I'm at the Reece place over on Lily Pond Road—"

"The estate?"

"Right. We had an ambulance call that didn't get to me until shortly after eight this morning—apparent drowning. Should have gotten the call by six-thirty but it went to the goddamn Vilas County Sheriff's Department where they've got a new hire on their switchboard who dicked around assigning it to all the wrong people. Then I lost an hour trying to locate goddamn Pecore, who neglected to mention to anyone that he and his wife would be spending the holiday in Minneapolis with their daughter."

Lew's voice had been rising as she spoke. Unflappable under most circumstances, right now she sounded as if every human being in the world on whom she depended had done their best to let her down. Later Osborne would learn that wasn't the only problem. The glitches and delays had made it impossible for Lew—who had awakened under the impression that she had the day off—to get her turkey in the oven.

"So you need a deputy coroner at the Reeces'?"

"Yes, Doc. That is what I need." And she didn't have to say how fast.

IN SPITE OF THE frustration in Lew's voice, Osborne's heart lifted. He loved it when she needed him. Of course that usually meant some poor soul had passed, so he had to temper the enthusiasm he felt whenever he got the call—a call that never failed to remind him that settled as your life may seem, things can always change.

It certainly never occurred to him during a stint in the military thirty-five years ago when he was assigned to assist a forensic dental detail, that such grim work might someday enhance his love life. (Nor did he ever anticipate having a love life at the age of sixty-three!)

But those six months of training were all the credentials he needed for Loon Lake Chief of Police Lewelleyn Ferris to deputize him. At first appointed deputy coroner in Pecore's absence, Lew later found it handy—given his thirty years of dentistry in tiny Loon Lake meant he knew many residents from the inside out—to enlist him as a full deputy when she was short-handed. And at the height of the hunting season in Loon Lake, a three-person law enforcement team was bound to be short-handed.

That early training added zest to his daily life as well. He might be retired from the rigors of Loon Lake's largest dental practice but he took care to maintain his membership in the Wisconsin Dental Society and attend their semi-annual workshop on forensic dentistry—a subject now formally recognized as the science of odontology.

Staying abreast of advances in the field continued to pay off as not even the Wausau Crime Lab was able to afford the full-time services of an odontologist. That budget issue guaranteed him access to Chief Ferris whenever their region yielded the remains of a hapless fisherman who suffered a heart attack while landing a 47-inch muskie, a hunter felled by a self-inflicted gunshot wound as he tumbled from a deer stand, or a snowmobiler too drunk to see a break in the lake ice.

It pleased Osborne, too, that over time Lew had made it clear she preferred to work with him—the guy she met in a trout stream the night he thought he had hired a fishing guide named "Lou"—rather than Pecore. And having decided to teach him that fly fishing was about more than just fishing—she refused to let him pay for instruction on how to cast a weightless trout fly.

Pecore managed to aid and abet their relationship with his own aberrant behavior—a pattern that combined a talent for disappearing without notice with so many DUIs that he was likely to be transportation-challenged when most needed. But no matter how hard he might work to compromise his duties as Loon Lake's appointed coroner—Pecore was in for life, the mayor was his brother-in-law.

"Doc, THE VICTIM'S family has been patient," said Lew as if she suspected he might be intending to finish a cup of coffee.

"I'm on my way. I'll stop by the house for my medical bag and be there within fifteen minutes. I know a shortcut off County C so it won't take long. Routine death certificate?"

"Umm…circumstances uncertain." The tone in her

voice changed, implying she didn't want to say too much given people standing nearby. "Todd is on his way and I've got a call in to the Wausau boys who are, of course, off for the holiday so who knows when they'll connect, but I've alerted St. Mary's we may be using their morgue."

Her tone was crisp and the signal clear: something was out of the ordinary. Had to be if she was pulling Todd Martin, her junior officer, away from his Thanksgiving table. And enlisting the Wausau Crime Lab on a national holiday? The Loon Lake municipal budget would be charged double for that. Osborne was intrigued. He forgot all about Kathleen and Fred.

SIX

"Jeez, Dad, what's all the excitement about?" said Erin, glancing up from where she was slathering a pale yellow sauce over steamed broccoli as Osborne walked back into the kitchen.

"Not sure exactly." He reached for the hunting jacket that he had hung over a kitchen chair. "Lew needs me out at the Reece place. There's been an accident—a drowning she said—and Pecore is AWOL, of course."

"Who drowned?" said Erin, wooden spoon midair and her face serious. "Anyone we know?"

"No idea. Lew didn't say. Doubt it though. Your mother used to talk about Nolan Reece. Sort of like Loon Lake royalty."

"Yeah, and I've been hearing a lot about the Reece place lately. They say the house is amazing." Opening the refrigerator, Erin bent to pull foil-covered dishes from inside as she said, "Better brace yourself—that Mrs. Reece is a piece of work."

"Why do you say that?"

"Observation. She's been in the Loon Lake Market a few times when I was there with the kids. And, Dad, I know I sound mean-spirited but to my eye that woman is big, she's loud, and you'd think she owns

Loon Lake the way she bosses people around. Just ask the poor guys behind the meat counter—according to her they can't do anything right."

"Oh? Maybe that's the problem," said Osborne. "Lew's asked the Wausau boys to help out, and you know how she hates to do that."

"The crime lab, huh. Must mean an autopsy. Well, isn't that interesting."

"Now don't jump to conclusions, kiddo," said Osborne, aware he may have said too much. Given his son-in-law was the assistant D.A., he didn't need to have Mark's office on high alert unless there was good reason. "Drowning is not considered death by natural causes so an autopsy is required regardless. From your description of Mrs. Reece, chances are she's demanding the experts—and that's fine."

Much as he loved his daughter, he knew not to say too much. News travels fast in Loon Lake and gossip always trumps facts.

Erin cocked an eyebrow. "I get the message, Dad. But be sure to look around while you're out there—I want a-a-l-l the details."

Bubbling on, she followed him through the living room as he headed for the front door. "Y'know a friend of Mark's did the stonework out there—he swears they put at least fifteen million into that property. Of course, that's easy to do when you sell the family business for a billion—give or take a few bucks. So, Dad," she called after him as he ran down the porch steps, "remember—you have got to tell me what that place looks like."

"I doubt I'll be looking at architecture," said Osborne. He paused as he reached the sidewalk. "Erin, honey, I'm sorry but I just realized there is no way I can make it back here in an hour…"

"That's okay, Dad. We'll have plenty of leftovers. Just stop by when you're done."

"Thanks, sweetheart, but that won't be necessary," he said, opening the car door. "Lew's invited me to her place for dinner at five. I'll get plenty to eat."

"D-a-a-d, you didn't tell me. You were going to eat two Thanksgiving dinners?"

"I didn't want to hurt your feelings."

"Get outta here—love you!" She waved as he drove off.

To Osborne's relief there was no white Lexus in his driveway. Kathleen and Fred must have left early. After letting Mike into the backyard and making sure the dog had water, he hurried through the kitchen to the den where he had to move a rack of fly rods that Fred had set in front of the cabinet where he kept his medical bag. Reaching for the bag, he heard a sound behind him.

Kathleen was in the doorway, her pug face pickled in cheeriness. "Paul," she said in a soft, eager voice, "we have to talk." Her conspiratorial tone prompted a flash of dread—was the house delayed another month?

"Not now, Kathleen, Chief Ferris just called me in on an emergency and…" Osborne started towards the doorway but Kathleen refused to move. "Excuse me," he said, angling one shoulder to slip past her. But the woman didn't budge. Instead she reached up to grasp his shoulders.

"This will only take a moment, Paul. Fred and I are leaving."

That was such good news, Osborne decided he could spare a moment to be gracious. "Oh, is the house ready? Isn't that a nice surprise." He waited for her to let go but instead she tightened her grip.

"No, Paul," she said, "the house isn't ready but Fred has a problem."

"He does?" Osborne turned back toward the den as if he might find Fred's problem in the piles of tools and materials still scattered around the room. As he turned, he pulled away, forcing Kathleen to drop her hands.

"He thinks we're having an affair."

"What?" Osborne was stunned. "That's awful—how could he possibly think that? Oh, Kathleen—I am so sorry. You want me to talk to him?"

She shook her head no, eyes half closed, then said, "I have a problem, too…Paul." Her hesitation, her caress of his name…Osborne waited, disbelief and worry over what might happen next commingling in his gut. "I know you're attracted to me and…Paul, dear heart, I feel the same for you…"

Kathleen's blue eyes, their lashes starched black with mascara, searched his. She took a step toward him. Osborne took two back, thinking hard. The woman was hallucinating. How could he save face for both of them?

"Paul, when you talk to me, when you look at me—your emotions just pour through your eyes…" She held her hands out, palms open in surrender.

For one frantic moment, he hoped this was all a joke. "Oh, golly, Kathleen," he said as he backed into the rack of fly rods, all of which slid sideways and tumbled to the floor, "I am very flattered but I should have told you—I am very, very involved with another woman. Very involved." He shook his head up and down to emphasize how incredibly involved he was.

"Oh, her." Kathleen waved a dismissive hand. "You mean that Lewellyn Ferris? She's not right for you, Paul. She's so…so rugged, so northwoods…and…and she doesn't have a graduate degree. I'm a social historian—you and I have so much in common—we're professionals. You're probably attracted to her because maybe she looks like your mother."

"What's wrong with 'northwoods'? I'm 'northwoods,' Kathleen. As far as my mother goes—she died when I was six. I barely remember her. How could Lewellyn Ferris possibly look like my mother?"

"I just said 'maybe,' Paul. But even her name is wrong—Lewellyn? That's a man's name. Now, Paul, it'll take time for us to work this out, I know. But I'm willing to wait, I feel so deeply for you…" The pug face swung back and forth.

"I've asked Lewellyn to marry me," said Osborne in a blurt of desperation. What he didn't say was that he had asked in jest and Lew had refused on the grounds that he had yet to set the hook in a twenty-two-inch brown. But the statement did the trick.

Kathleen stepped back. Her eyes narrowed. Obviously this was his mistake, not hers. "I wish you had told me."

"I know, I know, I should have," said Osborne, eyes sad and head shaking up and down as he did his best to take full responsibility for this horrible error. "But our plans are confidential—not even my daughters know. And I am so sorry if I have misled you."

"Well, you did. The way you listened to me with that deep, dark look in your eyes…"

"You're an educated, interesting woman, Kathleen. Perhaps at another time in our lives we might have—" He struggled for a kind way to say "no, no and NO."

The back door banged shut just then. "Have you told Fred?" whispered Osborne.

Kathleen shook her head. "I was hoping we would do that together." She moved sideways to let him pass.

Osborne, medical bag in hand, ran through the kitchen past Fred, who gave him a quizzical smile as he said, "Paul, did Kathleen tell you we've rented a cabin? Heard it advertised on 'Help Your Neighbor' and it comes with a heated workshop where I can build my rods—"

"She did—that's terrific, Fred." Osborne was out the back door. "I gotta rush—got an emergency down the road. Leave the dog in the yard—he's fine. Bye!" The door slammed shut behind Osborne. Never had he been so glad to have somewhere to go.

Minutes later, driving, he mulled over those painful moments with Kathleen…but Fred was so friendly— hardly the attitude of a man suspecting Osborne of having an affair with his wife. Kathleen must have made that up.

SEVEN

EIGHT FEET HIGH and crowned with a brass "R," a wrought-iron gate bordered with stone pillars guarded the entrance to the Reece estate. A security box with a dial pad and blinking lights hung over the drive, a warning to anyone looking to enter—but the gate stood open. So Osborne drove through, twisting along a narrow road that passed a tennis court, a shooting range and a putting green before ending in a circle in front of the Reece mansion.

The house—high, wide and rustic—had been restored in the style of the grand hunting lodges favored by the lumber barons of the late 1800s. But if the style was late 1800s, the materials were strictly post-2000.

What appeared to be a slate roof was in fact concrete, which Osborne recognized immediately. Mary Lee had desperately wanted just such a roof as a bragging point for their home. It took months of arguments, pouts and tears before she agreed that concrete was, for them, too costly. Not for the Reece family. As if to emphasize that expense, the edges of the impressive roof gleamed with copper gutters that had seen few winters.

He couldn't identify the wood used for the home's exterior. Whatever it was had been stained dove-gray—a dove-gray not natural to the trees of the north. Nor did the stones in the foundation, unusual in their patterns and colors, resemble any of the rock or boulders native to glaciated northern Wisconsin. No doubt imported—at significant cost.

Though he was in a hurry, Osborne couldn't help but notice the windows. The vertical lines echoed the height of the pines along the circle drive, glass panels meeting in seamless perpendiculars at each corner with not a post in sight: another architectural detail not offered at a discount.

Just beyond the house was a six-car garage hosting what appeared to be a convention of Land Rovers, different models but all the same sleek gray to match the house. Seeing no place to park, nor any sign of Lew's police cruiser, Osborne continued along the drive, which now ran beside a high stone wall. Even though he slowed as he rounded a sharp curve, he nearly rear-ended a parked pick-up truck. A battered blue pick-up with a shiny 14-inch walleye leaping from its hood. The very pick-up that shuddered into his own driveway at least once a day.

Braking to a stop behind the truck, he spotted what his friend and neighbor would describe as "new and exciting additions" to the rusty bumper hanging cock-eyed off the back of his vehicle: "Honk if anything falls off," read one sticker. "If you can read this, I lost my trailer," read the next. Any other time Osborne might have chuckled. Not today.

LOON LAKE POLICE Chief Lewellyn Ferris did not deputize Ray Pradt unless she had good reason to employ a man whose misdemeanor file was thick enough to merit its own drawer. Even as state and federal penalties for smoking dope were easing, Ray was still a guy who could fire up the blood pressure of certain City Council members. That, plus his habit of poaching private water, kept the game warden on his tail as well—and only enhanced his reputation among certain Loon Lake locals who lived down lanes with no fire numbers.

Eventually the mayor and his cronies would calm down and approve the hiring of the man known to be the best tracker in the region. Keen-eyed, quick and as alert as a deer—the joke over coffee at McDonald's was always "that Ray Pradt can go into a revolving door behind you and come out ahead."

But that wasn't his only talent. You had only to drive down the street behind the blue pick-up and watch everyone wave at its driver: from the MDs who had practiced with his father to the lawyers who'd gone to school with his sister to the kids whose worms he judged during the annual Loon Lake Worm Race and the nuns he charmed with stringers of fresh-caught bluegills. Not least among his pals were the miscreants whom he had entertained with bad jokes while spending random nights in the Loon Lake jail.

"You want to catch a crumb bum, you gotta think like a crumb bum," Lew would say when arguing her case to hire the guy. "Ray can do that. I'm not saying he is a crumb bum—but he knows 'em all. And if he doesn't know the one we want—he'll find someone who does.

And that, gentlemen, is what we pay for—Ray Pradt flips pancakes for people you and I never even see."

And while Ray could try Osborne's patience with the dumb jokes and stories that went on w-a-a-a-y too long, the older man endured the antics of his neighbor, thirty years his junior, with respect and affection. After all, Osborne owed him. It was Ray who had watched and waited for the right moment to talk Osborne—so deeply depressed after Mary Lee's death that his cocktail hours had started at noon—into the meetings behind the door with the coffeepot on its frosted window.

Lewellyn Ferris's final argument in favor of hiring Ray was always the same: "That guy's got the ears of a wolf—he can hear a cloud pass by." But she was only half right. Osborne knew that the driver of the battered blue pick-up with the walleye leaping off its hood could hear beyond the whispers in the sky. Tuned to the desperation that can cloud a heart, he was the person to whom Osborne owed his self-respect, if not his life.

As Osborne walked quickly past the blue pick-up, a long arm in a rust and green plaid sleeve waved from the window. "Doc, tell Chief I'll be right there," said the driver, pointing to the cell phone glued to his right ear.

"I'd hurry if I were you," said Osborne, wondering for the umpteenth time how it was that a guy who lived in a house trailer and dug graves when money was tight managed to own the latest in electronic devices: a cell phone that rang with the sound of birds twittering, an iPod stuffed with vintage rock 'n' roll—and satellite radio in his bassboat! All that expensive gear even as Ray jury-rigged his plumbing to fertilize the roses planted by Mary Lee—an act that had so infuriated Osborne's late wife that if she hadn't died of a severe bronchial infection, apoplexy might have done her in.

Osborne shook his head. He knew the source of Ray's electronic surplus: women. The ladies he charmed, bedded and somehow managed to convert to "just friends" loved to shower him with gifts.

"Now how the hell does he do that?" was a familiar refrain among men who might fancy themselves wealthier and wiser—but were never so lucky.

OSBORNE HURRIED down the drive, now steep and curving on its way to a large boathouse. Beyond the boathouse he could see a wide, dark green deck that narrowed to a dock that jutted out over the water. An ambulance was parked next to the boathouse, and leaning up against it, arms crossed as they chatted with Deputy Todd Martin, the younger of Lew's two full-time officers, were two EMTs from St. Mary's Hospital. Osborne gave a silent wave as he rushed by.

Just beyond the deck and standing on the shoreline to one side of the dock was Lew Ferris, her back to him as he approached. She was engaged in conversation with two people—a tall, slim young woman with very short hair that stood stiffly on her head and a pudgy man of medium height who, in spite of the cold wind blowing off the lake, was wearing tan Bermuda shorts, a navy blue sweatshirt, black socks and sandals.

A crumpled khaki fishing hat had been crammed onto his head and under the hat was a round face heavy with jowls. Thick-rimmed glasses magnified his eyes, making them appear larger and darker than normal. As he registered the man's pudginess, the glasses, the shorts and the black socks—Osborne couldn't help thinking he looked like a nerdy school kid out of a Far Side cartoon.

The lanky girl standing beside the man, one arm tight across his shoulders and leaning forward as she listened to Lew, appeared to be in her early twenties. She was dressed for the weather in jeans, a black fleece jacket and hiking boots. It was the girl who spotted Osborne approaching and pointed his way.

Only then, as all three turned towards him and Lew stepped back, did Osborne see the dark figure lying at their feet.

EIGHT

"OH, GOOD, IT'S you, Doc," said Lew as Osborne walked up. She glanced down at her watch. "Say, you didn't happen to see—"

"Yes, I did. He's on his way down," said Osborne. "Taking a phone call—I told him to hurry."

"Thank you. It'll be dark in three hours and he needs to get started."

Osborne did not miss the grim resolve in her voice. Two years of assisting the Loon Lake Police Department on murder investigations had taught him Lew was convinced that "if you don't find your best evidence within the first 48 hours, you may never find it." Given that these late November days made for limited hours of good light, Ray better show up fast.

"Dr. Osborne, this is Andrew Reece, the victim's husband, and her daughter, Eleanor—"

"Blue, I go by Blue," said the girl, stepping forward to grab Osborne's hand with a grip so strong his knees nearly buckled. She was at least six feet tall, broad-shouldered and, if her handshake was any indication, a very strong young woman.

"Dr. Osborne," said her father, shaking Osborne's hand with a grip as limp as his daughter's was fierce.

"The name is Andy—only the IRS knows me as Andrew," he gave a weak smile as if embarrassed to be attempting humor but unable to resist, "so, please, call me Andy." His voice was one of those male baritones—fuzzy, deep and so low Osborne could barely hear him.

"I assume the victim is Mrs. Reece, and her first name is…?" asked Osborne as he knelt and reached into his black bag for a notebook and pen. He stood up, ready to listen.

"Nolan Marsdon Reece," said Reece with a quick shove at his horn-rimmed glasses. "I was just telling Chief Ferris I cannot count how many times I warned my wife not to go down near the dock when there was lightning—"

"Andy thinks she was hit by a rogue lightning strike," said Lew, maintaining a poker face familiar to Osborne: willing to listen, not likely to believe.

"You know a guy out fishing on Lake Tomahawk last month was hit. Not a cloud in the sky," said Reece. "Not a mark on him either until they opened him up—internal organs were…" the big eyes behind the dark glasses misted and the voice cracked as Reece said, "just…cooked."

"Well," Lew cut him off before he could say more, "no need to get all upset about things until we know exactly what we're dealing with here."

Osborne glanced down at the body lying on the sandy shore. As if wrung by giant hands, the woman's wet, black clothing was twisted tight along the length of her body, outlining sizable buttocks, a torso of significant diameter and broad shoulders. The legs, in contrast, were long and surprisingly slim: the classic apple shape that Osborne associated with people prone to heart attacks.

The corpse lay on its side, head turned away so he couldn't see the face. Stiff breezes had dried the shoulder-length salt-and-pepper hair, which was fluttering in the wind—the hair as active as the body was still.

"She was found in the water by Mr. Reece early this morning and he pulled her in to shore. She hasn't been moved since," said Lew, explaining the body's position.

"You tried CPR?" said Osborne to Reece.

"Ah, no. It was pretty clear to me that, ah, it was too late for that."

"I helped Dad pull her in," said Blue, stepping forward. "No question my mom was…" Her voice faltered.

DEAD IS A DIFFICULT word to use. Osborne knew that. At the hospital the night Mary Lee died, he had placed the call to each of his daughters but had to hand the phone to Ray when it came to delivering the unexpected news. Ray, who had awakened from a sound sleep to answer Osborne's frantic call for help in the middle of a raging blizzard; who had staggered through knee-high drifts to attach his plow to the pick-up and drive the Osbornes over snow-bound roads to the emergency room. Ray, whom Mary Lee had done her best to drive off his property because his trailer obstructed the views from the north side of her new deck, had not hesitated to help save her life. And it was Ray, one arm grasping Osborne's shoulders, whose gentle, calm voice had been able to pronounce that difficult word.

"Doc, I HAVE a sketch that indicates where Andy found the victim," said Lew with a wave of her notebook.

"Right there," said Reece, turning to point towards the dock. "She was floating just this side of that shore station with the bassboat—and about four, maybe five feet out from the dock…" He looked at his daughter for confirmation.

"Yes, that's where we found her," said Blue. "Our lake is so down that there's less than three feet of water there. That's why I don't think Mom drowned—so maybe Dad's right and it was lightning?"

"You can tell us for sure, Dr. Osborne," said Reece, "but I heard thunder off in the distance late last night. Lightning can strike without rain, you know. Like I said—my wife had a ridiculous habit of always coming down to the dock before she retired, no matter the weather—"

"Thing is—this is November," said Lew, interrupting. "We're more likely to get snow than rain. I don't recall any thunderstorms predicted for last night and weather is something I pay attention to. Our muskie season ends Saturday. With that plus opening deer season, I anticipate lots of traffic on the roads so I've been watching the forecasts.

"But enough conjecture. We'll know soon enough. Now, Dr. Osborne, will you please explain to Mr. Reece and his daughter what you will be needing from them."

"Certainly," said Osborne, as anxious as Lew to get the process underway. "First, I am responsible for documenting that a death has occurred—not cause of death. That's up to the pathologist and that could take some time, depending…" Catching a look of caution from Lew he decided to skip the usual patter on whether or not an autopsy would be required. Given she had made that decision in spite of the cost to her budget, he saw no need to open the issue for discussion. "…on their schedule," he wound up instead.

"As deputy coroner, my role is to confirm that a death has occurred, state whether it is natural or unnatural, and note the apparent circumstances. With your help, I'll complete an initial draft of the death certificate that will be finalized following the autopsy. And I believe," he turned to Lew, "that Chief Ferris has arranged for the autopsy…"

Lew nodded. "Yes, Mr. Reece is aware I've made those arrangements." Again the look of caution directed at Osborne.

"Please, please, Chief Ferris, Dr. Osborne, the name is Andy." Reece raised his voice to the booming level as he said, "The formality of 'Mr. Reece' is just… unsettling. No one who knows our family calls me 'Mr. Reece.'" He pushed at his glasses, jammed both fists into his pockets, and swayed back and forth on his sandals.

"Right, right, I'm sorry…Andy it is," said Lew with a quick, tight smile as she jotted a note into the narrow reporter's notebook that spent calmer days in her back pocket. "Andy…Blue——" Lew nodded towards each of them as she spoke "——once Dr. Osborne has examined the victim, the EMTs will handle the transport to St. Mary's. The deceased will be kept in the hospital morgue and I am sorry but you won't be allowed access until the pathologist has completed the autopsy."

"How soon will that be?" said Andy.

"Today's a national holiday, which delays things a bit, but I'm hoping to have it completed sometime tomorrow," said Lew. "When we'll have the results depends on the nature of any tests they may have to run." As she spoke, Osborne realized the reason for her cautionary looks: she did not want to disclose that the pathologist she had requested perform the autopsy was not one affiliated with the hospital but an expert from the Wausau Crime Lab.

"I'll let you know as soon as Mrs. Reece can be released to the funeral home. Will you be taking the remains back to Illinois?" Lew's pen was poised over her notebook.

Andy Reece looked at his daughter with a blank expression on his face. Again the push on the glasses. "What do you think, Blue?"

"Dad, she would hate that. We better wait and see if she put anything in her will about it. You know if we do it wrong…" Blue paused. Osborne couldn't help but think she had caught herself about to say that if they didn't follow orders, her mother would rise up in anger and rejoin the living. Blue's words hung in the air.

"Well, let me get started here—you people have waited long enough," said Osborne in a tone identical to the one he used to alert patients they would feel a slight prick as he injected a local anesthetic.

"Very good," said Lew. "Now, Andy and Blue, would you please wait for us up in the house? Don't anyone leave or come down here until we've finished. This shouldn't take long and then Dr. Osborne and I will come up and go over—"

"So you still need to talk to us even though we've told Chief Ferris everything?" said Blue, looking at Osborne.

"Yes, I will need information for the death certificate," said Osborne, "your mother's age, last birthday, place of residence and a list of her first-degree surviving relatives."

"And after Dr. Osborne completes his exam, I may have more questions for each of you as well," said Lew.

"I see," said Andy. "Blue, I'll need your help locating our family records in your mother's files—may have to call Vern Pokorny for some of that information."

"You mean Vern Pokorny here in Loon Lake?" said Osborne, surprised at the mention of a familiar name but also at the fact that Andy might not have the most basic information about Nolan right at hand. Were they not husband and wife?

"Vern handles all my wife's affairs locally and he's in touch with her legal team in Chicago, too," said Andy. "Certainly the news of her death—he needs to be told ASAP. This could affect the company stock price, you know. She may have sold the company but as a major shareholder…"

"I'd like you to hold off making that call," said Lew. "We don't need reporters out here."

"But it's only an accident," said Blue. "Why would they be interested?"

"Two reasons, Blue. Not only is your mother a prominent figure, but in a small town like Loon Lake even accidents are news," said Lew. "And for the record, young lady, we don't yet know how your mother died."

Blue looked from her father to Lew to Osborne. "But Dad said lightning."

"We don't know anything for sure," said Lew.

Blue stared at her, then asked, "Should we be afraid?"

"I can't answer that," said Lew. "Please, go up with your father and let us do our work here."

As Blue turned towards the stone stairs leading up to the house, she glanced past Osborne. A stunned look crossed her face. With a yelp, she bolted across the deck.

NINE

A PAIR OF VERY long legs in blaze orange hunting pants appeared to flicker as they descended the steep drive in quick, skidding steps. It was Ray at last, his six-feet-six inches advancing in a loopy rhythm: the lower half arriving split seconds ahead of the upper half.

It was the latter—the late half—that Blue clutched, burying her head in the collar of the green and rust plaid shirt as she broke into sobs. Wrapping his arms around her, Ray pulled the girl close. As they stood together, both so tall, so lanky, they struck Osborne as an unlikely but interesting duo.

Ray's deep tan along with his full head of auburn curls and beard (trimmed to what he called his "winter mode"—a modest four inches of more auburn curls, these laced with gray) contrasted with the girl's pale, lightly freckled face and the fawn-colored spikes gracing her head. Their age difference, which had to be at least ten years, wasn't easily apparent.

"Now how the hell?" Lew turned to Osborne in amazement. He shrugged. He had no idea how Ray might know the girl. Ray had certainly never mentioned her over morning coffee or during one of their lazy evenings in the boat that summer.

As they watched, Ray tipped his head close to Blue's right ear, murmuring words they couldn't hear. Wiping at her tears, the girl nodded as if to agree to whatever it was he'd said. Her father, observing the scenario in silence, pushed at his glasses, moved closer to Lew and Osborne and murmured, "I don't know that man, do you?"

"Yes, we do," they answered simultaneously, not taking their eyes off the couple as Ray gave the girl a hug, then released her with a pat on the back. Lew glanced over at Andy and said, "That's Ray Pradt, the deputy I hire to shoot photos for incident reports. What I'm wondering is how he knows your daughter."

As Lew spoke, Blue turned toward them in silence, waved to her father and hurried across the drive to the stone stairway leading up to the big house. Andy ran after her.

"Okay, fella, before you get started, I want to know how it is you know that young woman," said Lew, keeping her voice low as Ray walked up. In addition to his hunting pants and canvas vest, he wore a square camera pack slung across his chest. A smaller camera was attached to his belt. Ray gave a slow smile but said nothing, taking his time to remove the larger camera from its case.

ONE OF PECORE'S official duties as coroner was to photograph crime scenes, accidents and any other sites involved in an unnatural death. Osborne could handle the photography if pressed but it was Ray whose keen eyes complemented the camera lens in ways that had helped the Loon Lake Police find incriminating evidence in tire tracks and footprints that might have otherwise gone unnoticed.

But it was nature photography where he excelled and that he loved. He took pride in having shot photos good enough to be featured in a local insurance agency's annual calendar and, more recently, purchased by Ralph's Sporting Goods for use on their Web site. His series of Great Blue Heron photos often went for as much as ten bucks each on eBay!

As a result of Ray's modest commercial success and also due to the fact that Pecore refused to learn to use a digital camera, Lew now leaned on Osborne's neighbor to shoot crime and accident scenes even when Pecore was available. "He tracks with that lens just as he does with his eyes," she would say when challenged on the extra expense. More than once she had urged Ray to take up photography as a profession but he always had the same answer: "Nah, that would mean a full-time job. No way!"

"How do I know Miss Reece—is that what you want to know, Chief?" said Ray. "Oh…well." He paused, tipped his head to one side and raised an authoritative index finger. A bad sign: a signal that he was about to launch a lengthy discourse.

"Short version," said Lew, "we're running out of time. Be dark in a few hours." Osborne had to resist a grin. Good luck. Given the slightest opportunity to be the center of attention, Ray could stretch out his words and pepper his sentences with long pauses—excruciating for a listener in a hurry. But Lew, hands on her hips, eyes black with impatience, was not up for wasting one more minute.

"I hear ya, Chief. Fact is…the old lady hired me to guide them on that fancy pontoon of theirs," he gestured towards a pontoon boat barely visible in the boathouse off to the right. "I took 'em out a couple times this past summer. Blue's a sweet kid, but her mother…just obnoxious. Last time we went out she kept insisting that I wasn't taking them to spots that looked 'fishy' enough. I tried explaining structure and that the surface can be, y'know…misleading—but she wouldn't listen.

"Next she decides they have to switch over to fly rods 'cause the spinning rods aren't happening—some idiot told her she could catch muskies easier on a fly rod, and we know who that was, don't we…"

"Ralph," said Lew, trying to hurry the story along.

"Yeah, well, now…she makes me tie on these purplish blue Hotshots because the color matches the damn boat. Do we catch fish? N-o-o-o. So then…she pays me half what she owes b-e-e-cause her idea of a good day's fishing is an outrageous number of fish caught versus…my belief—"

"Romance, excitement and live bait—get it all fishing with Ray," said Lew, jumping in to finish his sentence.

"Oh, have I said that before?"

"Many times—you know that."

"Later, I took Blue out on her own—no charge—so she could experience a fine day's fishing without…the old lady interfering. Blue's okay, she's a good kid."

"All right, that makes sense," said Lew. "Now that I know your connection to the family can we get started here? I need you to shoot everything before anyone other than the three of us enters this area extending from the boathouse to both property lines."

"You got it," said Ray. Then, assured that Lew was satisfied with his answer, he turned sideways and shot Osborne a look, serious and sad, that said it all: Of course, that's not how he knows Blue Reece. But the rule is that only Blue can tell Lewellyn Ferris or anyone else how it is they know one another.

"Well, the mother happens to be problematic today, too," said Lew, stepping back to point towards the dark figure on the shore behind her.

"No-o-o." The surprise on Ray's face was genuine. "You're kidding. That's Nolan Reece?"

"JEEZ LOUISE, this gal kinda exceeds the design specs, doesn't she," said Ray as he helped Lew and Osborne gently roll the woman's body onto its back before taking more photos. "They're gonna need a custom cabinet for her."

He had a point. Not even the black of her clothing could diminish the woman's heft. Nolan Reece had carried her weight in her torso, which measured almost two feet from back to front. It wasn't that the woman was fat so much as big. Large-boned and fleshy as happens to affluent people who dine too well and savor the expensive in wine and spirits. Osborne had only ever glimpsed her from a distance, but enough to recognize that alive she had been an imposing figure.

"Well-dressed, wouldn't you say, Lew?" he asked, noting the victim's jacket, which was heavily embroidered and ruffled at the cuffs. One foot still wore a black flat shoe, shiny with sequins—the other was bare. Oddly, the clothing—both jacket and pants—was snagged in multiple places, leaving tiny, loose threads to wave in the breeze. Having seen wrinkled linens and crushed skirts in his daughters' wardrobes, Osborne wondered if snagged fabric was some current fashion statement.

"I'm sure it's very expensive clothing, Doc," said Lew. "The party the family gave last night was to announce the engagement of their daughter to a young man from Chicago. So everyone was celebrating until late. That's why Andy thought his wife had left the party and gone to bed, which she's been known to do after having a little too much to drink. He alleges that because they have separate bedrooms, he wasn't aware that she'd left the house.

"So, Doc, would you go ahead with the dental exam before the EMTs move the body, please?"

"Certainly. I wasn't sure you needed it given the family has identified—"

"I need it and I'll tell you why afterward."

As Osborne reached for his instrument bag, Ray moved back and out of the way. "This should only take a few minutes," said Osborne, slipping on a pair of Nitrile gloves. He knelt beside the body and reached to brush aside clumps of wet hair obscuring the face.

Death had left the eyes open and dull, the mouth gaping. Down the left side of Nolan Reece's head, starting above the temple, crossing the cheekbone and extending beyond the lower jaw was a reddish brown abrasion. Osborne felt along the outside of the jaw then slipped his fingers inside the open mouth. Where he expected to find teeth, he didn't. Where he did find teeth, they were loose. Too loose.

"Lew," said Osborne, his voice tense with concern, "you called Wausau, right?"

"Sure did. Why?"

"This is very strange." He looked up from where he was hunched over the still form and gestured as he spoke. "On this side of the jaw, the teeth have been loosened. Recently. I'll bet you the autopsy will show that happened before she died. See the length and general appearance of this abrasion? I think she was slugged with something long and hard like a bat, but with an edge to it."

"Not a lightning strike?"

"Lightning has nothing to do with what I see here. This injury is similar to what I've treated in hockey players who've taken a puck in the mouth. For the players, the good news was I could usually push those teeth back in so they wouldn't lose them.

"But that's not all. On the right side of her upper jaw, there's a large gap where a fixed bridge should be. We both know this is not a woman who would have been entertaining guests without her teeth. So my question is—where is her bridge?"

"Right," said Lew, satisfaction spreading across her face. "I'll show you where it is and now you'll know why I called you and Ray—why I went out on a limb

to call the Wausau Crime Lab on a national holiday."
She stepped up onto the dock and motioned for
Osborne and Ray to follow.

"Holy cow," said Ray as they walked out along the
dock. They passed the shore station holding the bassboat, its hull sparkling in the sunlight. The boat was
suspended so high over the water that it might have
been resting on stilts. "Man, is this lake down! They
must have to row out quite a ways before starting that
big outboard. You unwind that shore station and you're
practically on sand. Wow."

Osborne wasn't surprised. A two-year drought
across the northwoods had left many of the lakes
down. Only those that were spring-fed and not linked
to a river system were at normal levels. Loon Lake was
also down but not quite as bad off as this.

"See that?" said Lew, pointing to something in the
water just to the north of the dock. Osborne's eyes
took a moment to adjust to the dark water but then he
saw the object, the silver bands gleaming as they
caught sunlight: a fixed bridge with, he guessed, at
least three teeth attached.

"Ray, can you get a photo before we retrieve
that?" said Lew.

"Sure, Chief. But I've got a question for you first."
He pointed to the shoreline above the spot where the
bridge rested. "Are those your footprints all through
that area? Did you or Todd walk from the deck over to
the boathouse along the shoreline there?"

"No. I didn't let Andy and Blue walk around there,
either—though who knows what people did before I

got here. For the record, gentlemen, the family doesn't know I spotted that bridge. Since Andy swears he found her body on the other side of the dock…"

"Chief," said Ray, "if it's okay with you, I'll shoot everything in color but let's do black and white around those footprints—you'll get stronger definition in case you need to identify shoe or boot marks."

"Good. And if those tracks lead farther back—"

"I'll stay with them?"

"As best you can, Ray." Lew cupped her hands to her mouth. "Officer Martin!" She waved at the young policeman who was still chatting with the EMTs. He hurried over.

"Todd, without question we have a crime scene here so will you please follow procedures? I don't expect Wausau to make it up here today, maybe not until morning. Sorry to ruin your holiday but we need to keep the area secured overnight, too. I'll check with the sheriff and see if I can get you a relief. But, please, let's be very careful to maintain the integrity of the site as well as the transport of the victim."

Todd nodded. "Not to worry, Chief. I know the drill. And the guys on duty today," he nodded towards the ambulance, "they know what they're doing. We've worked together before. They understand 'chain of custody' on crime scenes."

"Good. Doc and I will be with the family up at the house if you have questions."

Lew and Osborne walked back over to the body. Osborne paused to let his eyes travel the length and width of Nolan Reece. Torn flesh on the one hand that lay palm down caught his eye. He knelt to check the right hand, then the left.

"Lewellyn—take a look at this."

Lew dropped down beside him and leaned forward to closely examine the hands. The fourth finger on the left hand wore a large diamond ring but the nails on all five fingers, even the thumb, were ripped and torn. Same on the right hand: the fourth finger wore a large red stone in a gold setting but again, on every finger, the nails were torn.

Without looking up, Lew said, "Doc, I don't need a microscope to see scrapings under these nails. She put up a struggle, that's for sure."

"It's as if she was buried alive…"

"Yeah, but in water?"

"I know. It doesn't make sense."

TEN

"Doc, I know—I know—everyone grieves in their own way, but what bothers me…" Muttering as they trudged up the stone stairs leading to the lakeside deck of the main house, Lew was talking as much to herself as to Osborne. He waited for her to finish her sentence but if she did the words got lost in the wind.

A late afternoon cold front had kicked in with an edge that turned the sky pewter and the air icy. Branches crowning the tall pines that surrounded the house tossed in fury as winds out of the north roared over-head. Hunching his shoulders, Osborne pulled the collar of his hunting jacket up around his neck. "You warm enough, Lew?"

She didn't answer. Instead, near the top of the stairs, she stopped and turned towards Osborne. "Doc, how many hours have I been here?"

Before he could attempt an answer, figuring she knew better than he exactly how long it had been, Lew answered her own question: "Over six hours. And do you know that during all that time not once did I see Andy Reece or his daughter approach that poor woman's body? Those two kept their distance the entire time. And I mean distance—at least twenty feet away. Not once did I see either one of them make the slightest attempt to say a final goodbye—not a touch, not a whisper. And for a woman who's been so much a part of their lives?" She shook her head in disbelief.

"When it happened to me," said Lew, pressing her right hand, fingers spread, against her chest, "when I saw my son lying on that slab in the hospital morgue? I couldn't help myself. I gathered him up in my arms..." Her voice cracked, eyes glistening, and Osborne knew the memory of her son's murder at the age of seventeen had just hijacked her heart.

"Take a deep breath," he said, his own voice gruff, "I know what you're saying, sweetheart—we've both been there."

HE WOULD NEVER forget those first moments after the emergency room doc had entered the waiting room to tell him all was lost. Mary Lee lay on the gurney, her hair a tangled mess. He had reached to smooth back the strands with his fingers, knowing she would hate for anyone to see her so disheveled, knowing it was all he could do for the woman who had borne his children. One nurse, observing his attempt to comb with his fingers, found a hairbrush and together they brushed and tidied Mary Lee's hair and face. Only then, with a light kiss on the forehead, did he wish her Godspeed.

"I'M NOT SAYING they didn't pay lip service to the awfulness of the situation," said Lew, getting a grip, "but Doc, I've seen more attention paid to a dead bear, for God's sake."

"Before you arrived maybe…"

"Possible. Yes, I'm sure you're right. In the privacy of those first moments, you mean? It's just…for the average family to find their mother, their wife, dead under any circumstances is such a shock to the system. You know yourself how often I deal with folks who are inconsolable. Not these two. Very cool, very calm.

"Oh, well." Lew shrugged. "Andy did tell me that both their families emigrated from Sweden—her great-grandfather and his grandmother. Could be the Reeces are just more stoic than the rest of us." She started back up the stairs. "All right, let's get this over with."

WATCHING LEW AS she spoke, Osborne remembered Kathleen's words: "She's too rugged, Paul…"

Rugged? At the moment, Lew appeared less rugged than ragged as fatigue tempered with determination swept across her face: it had been a long day and it wasn't over yet. Still, Kathleen was right. Lewellyn Ferris was rugged, even tough. But the sight of those black eyes, the rogue curls clouding her forehead, the set of her wide shoulders over a body less slim than firm always stirred him.

And in spite of the day's stress, at the moment she looked particularly good. She had transitioned from the Loon Lake Police Department's summer khakis to their winter uniform: tan gabardine pants with a short jacket to match and two holsters planted firmly on each hip—one holding a cell phone, the other a 9-millimeter Sig Sauer pistol. To Osborne's eye, the uniform fit Lew's five feet seven inches just snug enough, especially where it left no doubt the Loon Lake Chief of Police was female.

She wasn't a small woman but medium-boned and sturdy. Muscular arms and legs served her well when scrambling up from trout streams in waders and a well-equipped fishing vest (that weighed at least five pounds) while manipulating a fly rod and, often, a cooler filled with bottles of water and cans of soda along with a sandwich or two, fruit, cheese and crackers —a cooler she always refused to hand over.

Rugged? Well, Lew Ferris was the only woman he knew who could carry a 100-lb outboard motor in one arm with only a slight lean to the left. But he knew, too, that her hair always smelled of a summer afternoon.

She was definitely tough-minded. As rigorous in her study of a criminal investigation as she was of a trout stream—always listening, watching, taking time, taking care—no detail unobserved. Working alongside Lewellyn Ferris over the last two years had taught Osborne a couple of simple but critical facts: that streetwise beat book-wise, that a true professional learns on the job.

Okay, he would concede to Kathleen. But where she saw rugged, he saw a swan.

"...To TELL YOU the truth, it was more like they were relieved than grief-stricken," he heard Lew say.

"What's that? You say you sensed relief?" Osborne's mind had wandered.

"I'm not sure what I sense at this point. Talk about

a long, frustrating day and, Doc, we'll have to go out for dinner because I never did get my turkey in—"

"Did I hear…t-u-r-r-r-key?" Ray bounded up the stairs behind them. "Chief, with the light fading so fast, I'm finding it difficult to track into that cedar swamp that runs along the edge of the property. The footprints along the shoreline head up in that direction but right now there are too many shadows. If it's all right with you, I'll get a good start first thing in the morning."

"I think that's wise," said Lew. "Todd is securing the area and the Wausau boys will be here by then, too."

"Now what's the problem with your turkey? I've got a nice twelve-pounder roasting away and I'm happy to share if—"

"Hey, that's a thought," said Osborne. Ray's cooking more than made up for the frustrations he caused his friends—plus Osborne knew he had recently acquired a stash of native wild rice and native always tasted better than store-bought. "Lew?"

"I did get my pies baked," said Lew, "pumpkin, apple and a blueberry tart. And my butter rolls. Sure—this is a great idea. If you don't mind driving out to my farm, Ray, my table is set and I'll just add one more place setting. How does seven work for you?"

"Well…on one condition…"

"Y-e-e-s?" said Osborne and Lew with mutual trepidation.

"I'm allowed to bring a guest."

"Oh…" Again they responded in concert. Ray had a habit of lending a helping hand—or a free night on his sofa—to men temporarily down on their luck. This was a good thing except some were so peculiar in their appearance that they could frighten young children. Or alarm a retired dentist who had difficulty dining with people possessing less than ten teeth. The turkey was enticing but…

Osborne locked eyes with Lew as they assessed the risk. "Sure," said Lew after a moment, "after all, it is Thanksgiving. If you don't mind trucking over that turkey, I'm happy to include your friend—but only one, right?"

"Only one, I promise. And I'll make gravy at your place."

As Ray tripped back down the stairs, Osborne said, "I hope it is only one—he's said that before and shown up with a gaggle."

"Oh, what the hell," said Lew with a chuckle of surrender, "this day has been bizarre from the get-go."

As THEY WALKED around to the front of the house, they were startled to see a van drive through the circle and pull up next to an entrance on the side of the house. A slightly overweight woman in tan slacks and a black ski jacket jumped out. She had a square, friendly face and wore her long red hair pulled back into a ponytail. She looked familiar to Osborne but he couldn't think of her name.

Whoever she was, she was so intent on what she was doing that she didn't notice Lew and Osborne standing less than fifty feet away. Sliding back the side door of the van, she pulled out a small dolly, which she yanked into shape before reaching back into the van.

"Excuse me—" said Lew, stepping forward.

Startled, the woman jerked around. "Ohmygosh you scared me!"

"I'm sorry," said Lew, "but visitors aren't allowed at the moment."

"Oh," said the woman with a wave of her hand and a cheery smile, "I'm not a visitor, I'm the caterer. I've got the Reeces' Thanksgiving dinner here. Oh, Dr. Osborne!" The surprise in her voice escalated.

She thrust a hand towards Osborne. "Karen Gilley. I was your daughter Mallory's Girl Scout leader and my mom and dad were patients of yours—my maiden name was Carlson. Ruth and Gil Carlson, do you remember them? They both passed a couple years ago."

"Sure," said Osborne. "I knew them from St. Mary's, too." Of course, now he remembered.

Karen turned her friendly eyes back to Lew only to have it dawn on her that she was talking to a police officer. She threw a questioning look at Osborne, the smile fading. "What…"

"There's been an incident and we're conducting an investigation," said Lew, showing her badge. "Lewellyn Ferris, Loon Lake Chief of Police and I'm afraid the family is sequestered."

"Yes, Chief Ferris, I certainly know who you are. Oh, well, in that case may I just tell Mrs. Reece I'm here? She gets furious if I'm late."

"Karen," said Lew, her tone cautious, "Mrs. Reece is deceased. It happened earlier today but in consideration of the family's need to notify close relatives, her death won't be officially reported until later. Now I need you to keep this news in confidence and not mention it to anyone until tomorrow morning. Agreed?"

"Yes, oh, yes, of course." The friendly eyes turned worried, preoccupied.

"Karen," said Osborne, seeing the concern on her face. "I'm sure Chief Ferris can arrange for you to complete this delivery."

"It's not that. Oh, I feel terrible. This is such a selfish thought."

"What is it?" said Lew.

Karen looked sheepish as she said, "I'm just wondering if I'm going to get paid is all. Mr. Reece gave me a check last night but it covered only half of what they owe me counting today's order and another one she hasn't paid me for. Oh," she paused, "so that's why he paid me. I wondered 'cause she doesn't usually let him write checks. At least not the checks for catering." With an embarrassed wave of one hand, Karen said, "Forget it—I'm ashamed of myself for thinking this way when someone has just died. Did she have a heart attack? I tried to tell her—"

"It's premature to determine the precise cause of death," said Lew.

"Oh, an accident," said Karen. Lew did not correct her. "Well, then…" Karen spun around towards the van, then turned back again. "I mean, what do I do now? Like with the food?"

Leaning back to read the lettering on the van, Lew said, "You're 'Gilley's Catering'—all the way from Rhinelander I see."

"Yes. My business is based there but I live here in Loon Lake. I have a commercial kitchen in both locations. We did the party last night, too, but today it's just me dropping off their turkey and the fixings. I wasn't planning to stay…"

"You were here last night?" said Lew.

"Yes…" Karen's tone was tentative, as if hoping that wasn't a bad thing.

"Well, Karen, if you don't mind, Dr. Osborne and I would like to ask you a few questions about the evening."

"Sure, but why Dr. Osborne?" Karen looked more confused. "I thought you were a dentist."

"I'm retired from my practice—"

"But only from his practice," said Lew, interrupting. "The Loon Lake Police Department is working hard at keeping Doc busy. Given his experience in dental forensics, he has been kind enough to serve as deputy coroner on occasion—and he assists with interrogations when I'm shorthanded. Today being a national holiday, I'm shorthanded." Lew grinned at Osborne. "He's been a good egg to help out."

"Second career, huh?" said Karen, relaxing. "That's me, too. Spent twenty years teaching middle school, but this is a lot more fun. Here, let me close the van door so I can keep the food warm while we talk."

ELEVEN

"IF IT HELPS, I know everyone who was here last night," said Karen, her face flushed but eager. "Even though Mrs. Reece said she'd sent fifty invitations, we only had twelve for dinner—the Reeces, of course, then Barry—he's Blue's fiancé—and his folks, the Murphys, and six more guests. Oh—plus myself and the two people helping me."

"And is that everyone who was on the property last night?" said Lew.

"What about a clean-up crew?" said Osborne.

"We handled that. When I cater an event it's turnkey—everything from start to finish. Every last coffee cup and wineglass washed before we leave. Now, Chief Ferris, I can give you the names of all the guests, too. We made up place cards and that list is in a basket on the desk in the Reeces' kitchen—right through that door," she said, pointing.

"Was Mrs. Reece upset that she sent all those invitations but so few people came?" said Osborne. Mary Lee would have been apoplectic if that had happened to her.

"Not really. She knew when she sent the invitations that most of the Lake Forest people wouldn't be able to make it. I mean, it was the night before Thanksgiving. 'But I get credit for the invitation' is how she put it. Frankly, I think she planned the party for that night on purpose. For all her money, Nolan Reece can be tight about the strangest things."

"Karen, if you think back over the evening was there anything unusual?" said Lew. "Mrs. Reece's behavior? Did she spend a lot of time with anyone in particular? Did she seem worried about anything? What about the guests—any one of them out of kilter?"

"Um-m-m." Thrusting her hands into the pockets of her windbreaker and leaning back against the van, Karen mulled over the questions. She shook her head. "Y'know, not that I was aware—and I've catered a number of parties here. Memorial Day, the Fourth of July.

"It tends to be the same crowd if that's significant— her lawyer, her stockbroker and their wives. Then there's always Barry's mother, Miriam. His father not so often. Mr. Murphy's quite elderly and has trouble getting around. But Miriam always comes. She and Mrs. Reece are best friends—I guess they grew up together." Karen gave a sudden snort. "If you ask me, there's a reason it's always the same crowd—these are the only people I know who can get along with the woman."

"And what does that mean?" said Lew, looking up from her notepad.

"Nolan Reece is not easy to be around. Sure she's smart and wealthy and all that but she's…she's difficult."

"A bully? A know-it-all?" Osborne prodded. "'Difficult' can mean a lot of things, Karen."

"Well—" Karen pursed her lips as she considered

the question "—not sure quite how to put this, but she is—I mean was—always watching with this critical eye. And, brother, you do something the least bit wrong and she was in your face. She about ripped the head off their caretaker yesterday morning just 'cause he was blowing leaves and a few landed on one of those expensive cars of theirs. You'd of thought he'd shot one of the dogs or something. Poor guy. And he thought he was doing her a favor.

"Then she went off on me because I wasn't washing the lettuce right. That kind of behavior wasn't unusual either. Frankly, if I didn't need the business…" Karen rolled her eyes.

"She sounds insufferable," said Osborne. The "critical eye" comment had resonated with him. Why hadn't he seen that in Mary Lee before he married her? Thirty years of walking on eggshells—thank goodness those days were over.

"Yes and no—some people get along with her just fine. They know how to handle her. Sorry, guess I should say they knew how to handle her." Karen wrinkled her forehead in apology. "Hard to believe she's not here anymore."

"You said her lawyer, her stockbroker, her best friend," said Lew. "What about Mr. Reece? Aren't these people also his friends?"

"I'd say they're friends of the family. But he's odd."

"Now that you really have to define, Karen," said Osborne with a light chuckle. "Living here in the northwoods, you and I both know many folks who might be described as 'odd.'"

Karen gave a quick glance towards the side door before answering.

"It's okay," he reassured her. "I'm keeping an eye out."

"Andy Reece—and I think it's weird how he insists you call him by his first name even if you don't really know him—is s-o-o-o quiet. He's like a ghost in the house. I don't know that I've ever seen that man smile and he's always on his computer or watching ESPN2 in the den with the door closed—at least as far as I can tell.

"The few times he's come into the kitchen when Nolan is there, she stops what she's doing and stares at him until he leaves. Once she told me she hated him. The way she said it, she wasn't kidding." Karen threw her hands up. "How's that for a happy family?"

"Did she say this recently—about hating her husband?"

"When I was here on the Fourth of July. Not that long ago."

"Let's go back to the people at the party last night. You made the comment these people are the only ones who knew how to get along with—"

"Please," said Karen, one hand up as if to stop the conversation, "keep in mind I'm only telling you what I've observed during cocktails and dinner on a few occasions. I'm a small town girl, my opinion is hardly expert."

"I realize that," said Lew. "But you're helping Dr. Osborne and myself understand the dynamics here. And we'll be talking to other people—so, go on, tell us what you think."

"I told you she was critical. The other thing is you

cannot disagree with her. That's just asking for trouble. So, like last night? She was the center of attention and everyone seemed happy to sit back and let her run the show. That's how it always is. And why shouldn't they do things her way? I'm sure she pays them well.

"Of course, if you're the hired help and not a lawyer or a stockbroker then it's a different story. I'm a good example," said Karen with an ironic smile. "Her whole reason for hiring me was my reputation. She found out about me at a party Miriam Murphy gave at their summer place on Sunset Lake where everyone raved about my garlic-stuffed tenderloin and my pan-fried walleye with a crushed almond crust—but would she ever order those? No. Her recipes are better. She would tell her guests that, too," said Karen, mimicking Nolan: "'Karen thinks she does a mean steak but our Reece family classics are s-o-o much more delicious.'"

"And are they good?" asked Lew.

"Heavens, no. Same old steak and fish you can get anywhere. Plus she insisted I buy the ingredients wherever they were cheapest—and you better believe she went over those receipts."

With a shrug of resignation, Karen said, "Y'know, at first I had to fight the urge to tell her to do it herself but as I got to know her, I could see she was that way about everything. Sometimes she knew when she'd gone too far. The dinner party might have been about that. I know she was working hard to make it up to her daughter since she was forcing her to marry that boy."

"Oh, come on now," said Osborne. "That girl doesn't look like you could force her into anything.

Karen, I have two daughters and I can't imagine having any influence when it comes to the men they choose."

"Not to offend you, Dr. Osborne, but I doubt you have a multimillion-dollar trust to hold over their heads."

"Ah, so money has something to do with Blue's engagement?" said Lew.

"Certainly does." Even as she uttered the words, an emotion flashed across Karen's face. It lasted less than an instant but Osborne knew what he'd seen: worry that she'd said too much. "So, now that I've told you all this—do you mind telling me how she died?"

"The precise cause of death won't be known until an autopsy is performed," said Lew, dodging the question. "Now, why would Nolan Reece be forcing—"

"Oh, jeez, I don't want to get anyone in trouble and I shouldn't have made that crack about the engagement."

"Karen, please, you do not want to withhold any information that might help this investigation. That could prove troublesome…for you." Lew was gentle but firm.

Karen's face crumpled and she sagged against the van. "I'm not the person who should be telling you this," she said, tears welling in her eyes.

Lew studied her face, then said, "Can I count on you to keep some information confidential?"

"Yes," Karen said in a whisper.

"Right now," said Lew, "the circumstances of Nolan Reece's death are uncertain, which is why we have an immediate need to know what you know."

"Uncertain as in maybe it wasn't an accident or a heart attack?"

"Correct."

"Oh, dear…oh, my God." Karen covered her face with both hands and for a long sixty seconds she did not answer. Then, with a deep sigh, she dropped her hands and reached into her pocket for a Kleenex. She wiped at her nose.

"The boy Mrs. Reece insists Blue marry? He's gay."

"Oh," said Lew, her tone non-committal. "Does Blue know that?"

"Of course. All the kids know. So I don't think I'm telling you anything you won't hear from other people. Blue, by the way, is a wonderful girl. She's put up with a lot. A lot."

"So how is it the kids know this? And how is it you know?" said Lew, flipping her notepad open to a new page.

"My son told me. He bartends."

"Oh," said Lew, voice flat. "I hope this isn't the usual northwoods bar room sociology." A confused look on Karen's face prompted her to add, "As in you heard it from the bartender who heard it from a patron who heard it from his cousin while they were having a drink. It would be nice to have a more reliable source."

Karen's chin thrust forward as she said, "My son bartends at the Hodag Inn in Rhinelander full time during the week but weekends and holidays he helps me with the catering. He met Barry here at the Reeces' when we did the Memorial Day picnic…" Lew and Osborne waited.

"And…?" Lew finally spoke.

Pushing herself away from the van, Karen straightened up. Standing with her feet apart and her shoulders back, she crossed her arms as she said, "My son, Jason, is gay. He fell in love with Barry. And vice versa—they're a couple—and it's Barry who told him the whole story."

Karen's attitude shifted from friendly to fierce as she said, "Chief Ferris, Dr. Osborne, it is very important that you understand that I love my son and I respect him and I respect the relationship he has with Barry."

"Well..." said Lew, "that must complicate things for Blue, I imagine."

"Yes and no. Blue's mother simply refuses to believe that Barry is...who he is. And his mother doesn't help—she would love for her son to marry Blue."

"For the money?"

"I guess—though the Murphys are quite wealthy. They own car dealerships all across Illinois. What Barry told Jason is that Blue is supposed to inherit a twenty-million-dollar trust from her grandfather on her twenty-third birthday. However, her mother controls the trust. She told Blue that she could change the terms so Blue would get nothing until age thirty and even then she could change it if Blue doesn't—"

"Marry this young man," said Lew.

"Do what she tells her to, yes. The wedding is planned for next May. Just before Blue turns twenty-three."

"They're going ahead with this? For the money?" said Osborne.

"That's what Jason thinks. All Barry will say is that he and Blue have a pact. A promise they made to each other long ago. Has to be the money, don't you think?"

They heard a click and the door to the kitchen opened as Blue let herself out sideways, her back to the group standing near the van. She turned with a startled look. "Karen! I didn't hear you drive up—"

Before Karen could respond, Lew said, "Blue, please get your father. We have some important matters to discuss."

"Karen, why are you here?"

"Your mother ordered Thanksgiving dinner—didn't she tell you?"

"Blue, please, get your father," said Lew, stepping between Karen and the girl.

"I'll wait here," said Karen, climbing back into the van.

TWELVE

OSBORNE FOLLOWED LEW through a small foyer fronting a kitchen that was very spacious, very white and outfitted with stainless steel everywhere. Andy was seated at a round oak table that was tucked into a bay window overlooking the lake. A cup of something hot steamed alongside a laptop computer. Andy, eyes glued to the computer screen, did not look up as they walked in.

"I've got the information you need for the death certificate," he said, fingers tripping away on the keyboard. "Except—" he appeared to hit Save before looking up at Lew and Osborne "—for one thing." Shoulders hunched and squinting as if in pain, he said, "There is one issue we need to discuss in private, Chief Ferris...Dr. Osborne."

Blue gave her father a puzzled look. "You mean you want me to leave the room?"

"Just for a few minutes, hon," said Andy. "It's a private matter that was between your mother and myself, and I—she would want me to keep it that way."

"Well, sure, Dad," said Blue with a slight tremor in her voice. "I need something from my room anyway. Holler at me when it's okay to come back."

Andy waited until he heard her running up the stairs. "I've got a situation," he said in a whisper. "Blue doesn't know I'm not her natural father."

"That's not required on the death certificate," said Osborne. "Only the names of immediate survivors. Are you saying she's adopted?"

"Yes—by me but not by her mother," said Andy. "Does that have to be recorded?"

Osborne glanced at Lew, perplexed. "I don't think so—not if it was a legal adoption. But let me check on that. Of course we'll keep this confidential."

"Andy," said Lew, "we have a serious problem that must be dealt with immediately. But let's have your daughter back in the room first."

"Blue," Andy called out in a loud voice, then got to his feet and walked into the hall to call up the stairs. "Blue, would you come down, please?"

"Andy, Blue," said Lew as soon as Blue entered the kitchen, "though we can't tell you the precise cause of death until an autopsy is completed, it appears that Mrs. Reece was assaulted in some manner."

"What!" Blue was stunned. She moved toward her father.

"I've called in the Wausau Crime Lab for assistance and they will be here early tomorrow morning along with myself and several deputies. In the meantime, your property is being secured as a possible crime scene and that, I'm afraid, includes the house. You'll need to find somewhere to stay tonight, possibly several days, until we can be sure we've secured all the evidence."

"So it wasn't lightning," said Andy, his voice guttural as he choked out the words.

Lew shook her head. "No, it was not. Now, Dr. Osborne has what he needs for the death certificate and the two of you have given me enough details of your activities last night that I can prepare draft statements for you to review tomorrow. Meantime, do you need help finding a place to stay tonight? We'll wait here for you to make arrangements and pack overnight bags. And as soon as possible, please. It's been a long day and everyone is tired and hungry."

"Dad, we can stay over at Barry's folks' place, I'm sure. They flew back to Lake Forest this morning. I'll call and see if that's okay."

"I'll call for you," said Lew, "because your phones need to remain here—and not be used."

"Our cell phones?" said Blue, astonished.

"Your cell phones, your computers—any personal communication devices. It all stays here."

"My computer, too?" Andy's shoulders sagged. "But I'm right in the middle—"

"Sorry, that's the law," said Lew. "By the way, have either of you noticed if there is anything missing from the house?"

Blue and her father looked at each other. "I haven't thought to look," said Andy.

"Me, neither," said Blue. "What kind of thing?"

"Just anything that may have caught your attention—anything unusual. Any doors or windows open early this morning that shouldn't have been?"

As the two shook their heads, there was a knock at

the side door. Opening the door, Karen called in, "Blue, Andy—the girls are here for Thanksgiving dinner. Did you forget they were invited?"

Lew and Osborne turned towards the open door in time to glimpse a dark green Ford pick-up backing away from where it had pulled up next to Karen's van to deliver its occupants. Standing behind Karen were two teenage girls, shoulders hunched against the wind. They were dressed in identical forest green wool jackets and long, dark skirts that flapped around their bare legs: the Dark Sky sisters, Frances and Josie.

OSBORNE PULLED INTO the clearing in front of Lew's barn shortly after seven. He was still feeling relieved to have arrived at his own home and found it empty. No Kathleen. No Fred. No fly rods and fly tying materials clogging his den.

He had changed quickly, fed Mike and, after letting the dog into the backseat, jumped into his car for the drive to town. Stopping briefly by Erin's house, he delivered the dog to three enthusiastic grandchildren. They were always happy when their grandpa visited Chief Ferris because Mike got to sleep over at their house with his friend, Dido, the family Weimaraner. Mike never complained.

THE FARMHOUSE THAT had been Lew's home since her divorce years ago was set at the top of a long, sloping lawn that led down to a small lake, a lake so small motorboats weren't allowed on it. The cold front that had moved in late that afternoon had banished any cloud cover. As Osborne approached Lew's doorway, he stopped to look up at a sky so clear he could see the Milky Way. Stars and stars and stars filled the sky.

Lew opened the door before he could knock and up on tiptoes gave him a quick kiss. "Hurry in, Doc, it's cold out there." She had changed into black slacks and a black turtleneck that highlighted her dark eyes and the vibrant glow of her skin. A green checked apron completed the picture, reminding Osborne that she wielded a whisk as deftly as a 9-millimeter.

"Don't you look marvelous," he said as he hung his jacket on a peg of an old oak coat-tree and turned to give her a quick hug.

OVER THE YEARS, and doing most of the work herself, Lew had removed interior walls so that when you entered her home you walked into a wide open space: the kitchen with a butcher block table and chairs was to the left, the living room with a comfy sofa, chairs and a ceramic pot-bellied stove to the right, and windows all around. The home felt warm, comfortable and lived in. Every time he entered, Osborne understood, kind of, why she would never leave.

Not even the trauma of having been stalked on her property months earlier by a woman determined to kill her could shake Lew's love for the little farm. "I'm a big girl, Doc. I work in law enforcement and there are people in prison because of me. They may choose to track me down some day. I know that and I'm careful but I need this place—my little lake, my barn, my garden, my workshop. It's me. Simple as that."

So their homes had become something they laughed about: how each enjoyed the other's but loved their own. And, Lew stressed, there is virtue in solitude. Osborne understood her but his daughters didn't. "Dad, we really think you two should get married," they would say, shaking their heads over the relationship. "You both love the outdoors, you love to fish together…" He didn't have an answer for that except that he was not willing to risk asking Lew and be turned down. The few times he had brought it up, kidding of course, she had grinned in return—as if it was worth a chuckle but nothing more. Osborne got the message: better not to know than have your heart broken.

"THANK YOU FOR the compliment," said Lew, smiling for the first time that day, "but I'll look better when I've had something to eat. Any sign of Ray and his turkey? If you'll mash those potatoes, I'll finish whipping the cream for the blueberry tart."

Even as she said his name, Ray's headlights came bouncing into view through the windows of the living room. Osborne set down the masher and together with Lew rushed over to watch through the window. "Jeez, I hope he's not bringing someone who just got out of the hoosegow," said Osborne under his breath.

"Oh, oh," said Lew, "that's not Ray's car! I wonder who—" She started towards the front door but Osborne caught her sleeve.

"Hold on, Lewellyn, I see Ray getting out of the passenger side and he's wearing that hat of his." Osborne sounded a warning.

"Oh, yeah?" said Lew peering through the window. "We know what that means, Doc—a woman. And that's okay with me—"

"So long as whoever she is, she didn't just get out of the hoosegow."

Lew punched him in the arm. "Hey, I just thank the Lord he didn't show up in that hat this afternoon…"

EVERYONE KNEW RAY'S hat—a stuffed trout anchored to a battered leather cap with fleece-lined ear flaps that he wore loose over his ears in cold weather—was his prized possession and his guarantee for getting attention from the opposite sex. Granted having a fish hovering between your ears might not strike many as a babe magnet—but on Ray it was charming. Of course, it didn't hurt that the face beneath the fish was tanned, handsome and quick to break into a happy grin.

They watched in silence as Ray opened the trunk and reached for a large dark object, which Osborne assumed was the roasting pan with the promised turkey. A petite figure, a dark shadow against the car, waited for Ray, then reached in for something rounded and flat on top. They approached the farmhouse.

"Oh, my gosh, it's Gina Palmer!" said Lew. "I had no idea she was in town." Hurrying to the door, she flung it open and with a happy laugh pulled the black-haired pixie of a woman into the room.

THIRTEEN

THE PERFECTLY ROASTED turkey sat on the sideboard—half the bird it had been when it arrived. Bowls of leftovers had been tucked into the refrigerator (with equal portions for Ray to take home) and the first round of dishes washed and dried. Steaming cups of coffee rested alongside the remains of the evening's desserts: plates of crumbs and berry smears.

Sitting at Lew's table—the glow of candles reflected in the faces of people he cared for as they ate, chatted and challenged each other in good humor—Osborne was happy. Sometimes life was just that simple.

"So, the next thing you know," said Gina, who had been holding court as the candles burned lower and lower, "my grad students and I—we get this contract with Bank One, which has branches across the Midwest, to work with their data and see if we can't discover the source of fraudulent credit cards that have been hammering them. Ha! Talk about a challenge."

Osborne had forgotten how tiny Gina Palmer could kinetically charge any room: the cap of sleek black hair bobbing as she talked, the husky hammer of a voice filling all available space, and her hands—long, slender fingers flashing to emphasize every point. She was a woman who blew words out her mouth so fast he could only wish he could hit Rewind and catch up.

OSBORNE AND LEW first got to know Gina Palmer several years ago when a young woman to whom she was close was murdered during a visit to Loon Lake. At the time, Gina was an investigative reporter on the Metro Desk for The Kansas City Star. She flew north to claim the body and ended up assisting with the investigation. She also fell in love with the northwoods and, on impulse, bought a cabin on Loon Lake not far from Doc and Ray.

"Better investment than my 401 K," she would crow every time she sat on her dock with glass of wine.

In recent years, as the Internet changed the newspaper business, Gina moved on to specialize in "new media"— becoming an expert on using the computer, telecommunications and database research for investigative work. Fired up by the enthusiasm of young journalists, it was natural for her to migrate from the newsroom to the university classroom. Though academic life involved a lot of travel, she made sure the little cabin on the lake appeared on her itinerary every four months or so.

When in town, she always made it a point to update the computer techs servicing the Loon Lake Police Department with the latest online and database investigative tools—and never charged for her time. But the generosity went both ways, as Ray lent his services as caretaker of her property while Doc and Lew took turns educating her to the subtleties of fishing—on water and in water.

"I DON'T UNDERSTAND," said Osborne. "I thought that if you alerted your bank to fraudulent charges on your credit card, you weren't liable."

"You aren't," said Gina, "but the bank issuing your card is. And, in this case, Bank One branches are looking at a combined loss of three hundred thousand dollars over eighteen months and no clue as to who, where or why.

"They tried to see if there was any pattern to the stores where the cards were being used but it was happening all over Wisconsin and parts of Minnesota and Illinois. No defined pattern unless you call random a pattern."

While she talked, Osborne got up from his chair, walked into the darkened kitchen area for the coffee pot and returned to freshen all four cups. Eyes riveted on Gina, no one stopped him.

"So next they looked at whether goods were bought online or by phone—hoping to find a shipping address, of course—but everything was purchased on-site and walked right out the door—no trail. And that is when they came to me."

"How did they find you?" said Lew. "If we were dealing with the problem up here, I would never think to go to a university, much less a school of journalism for help."

"A former grad student of mine who had taken my data forensics course was working in their PR department. She suggested they have us do an initial analysis, which we did. And, boy, were the students fired up, too. A real life situation? Man, they were so excited.

"We started by constructing a database of the cardholders allegedly making the purchases. These appeared to be real people but even as the names were real, the addresses were real and the Social Security numbers were real—the card users making these particular purchases were bogus. The crooks, who we think may be a ring operating out of Canada, are very adept at mixing legitimate and phony data on credit cards in ways that fool banks and retailers. What made it even more difficult was that there were never more than two or three charges on a card in a single day. That limited use made the card users virtually untraceable.

"Knowing that much, we conducted a telephone survey to determine any similarities among the legitimate card owners—recent travel, where they shopped, that kind of thing. And you'll never believe what we found…" Gina pounded the table with her index finger as she enunciated each word: "Doc, Chief Ferris, Ray—every one of those people whose names were on those cards had vacationed or taken a business trip to Wisconsin within the last two years." She sat back, eyes sparkling with satisfaction.

"This far north?" said Ray. "You're kidding, right?" Gina shook her head, letting her words sink in. "Ah," said Ray, "so that's why you're in Loon Lake this weekend. And here I thought it was all about me."

"You're the icing on the cake, sweetie," said Gina, reaching over to pat his arm. But as Ray opened his mouth to respond, she held up her right hand. "Let me finish. We went back to the bankers with a proposal to fund three months of work: get a year of card purchases into the database, do more phone surveys and see what we got. And what we got was so surprising that when the analysis came in this past Tuesday, I booked a flight up here right away."

"Great," said Lew with a snort of a laugh, "so I start my day with a homicide and end with grand theft. Any other good news?"

"I don't think you have to worry about this," said Gina. "It's not Loon Lake but the state and the county that's our focus. Every cardholder we've spoken to happens to have bought a fishing license somewhere in this county. They might have been vacationing in the area, taking a break during the workday, up here for a fishing tournament. But the one thing they all did was purchase a fishing license."

"That'll take a few days to check out," said Lew. "Think of all the Mom and Pop bait shops and gas stations that sell fishing licenses. We must have dozens. Are you planning to go door to door with a list of names?"

"We've got tracking software that should do it," said Gina. "They all have computers that spit out the licenses after the data is input. We just have to find the right computer. So far the problem has been getting the ISPs on board."

"ISPs?" said Osborne.

"Internet Service Providers. They can identify the computer used for specific fishing license registrations. Once we clear the formalities with the ISPs' legal crews, it won't take long for us to find what we're looking for."

"Jeez Louise, you're going to put me out of the

tracking business," said Ray. "Between software and GPS, pretty soon no one will need eyes on the ground."

"Oh, I doubt that," said Gina. Then she slapped the table with both hands. "Enough about me, enough about my work. Tell me what's happening in Loon Lake these days."

TEN MINUTES LATER, having brought Gina up to date on miscreant hunters bagging too many ducks, over-served bar patrons and the investigation into the death of Nolan Reece, Lew sat back in her chair and exhaled. "We better call it an evening, folks. I have the Wausau boys arriving early tomorrow morning and a mountain of phone calls to make—starting with the people who were at that dinner party last night."

"Would you like me to follow up with Frances and Josie Dark Sky?" said Osborne. "I know the girls. Not well but they were patients of mine."

"That would be a huge help," said Lew. "But I'd like to sit in. I'm still wondering how they fit in the picture, aren't you?"

"Well, just before Karen offered to serve their Thanksgiving dinner at her own home—this was while you were walking Andy Reece through the lockdown of his property—Blue mentioned to me that her mother had worked out an arrangement with Mildred."

"Mind if I ask who you're talking about?" said Gina. "Sorry to butt in. My reporter instincts—I'm always nosy."

Osborne turned to Gina. "Mildred Taggert is an elderly woman who owns a small local grocery and has been the girls' foster parent for the last four years. Apparently Nolan took it upon herself to sponsor the girls—offer them a second family, provide financial support, buy clothes, pay for tutors—even college. According to Blue, the girls spend their weekends at the Reece home but live with Mildred during the week."

"Those sisters don't really look like sisters, do they," said Lew. "Frances is so tall and ungainly and that Josie is so petite."

A trill rang through the room and Lew jumped. "Oh, shoot, that's my cell phone. Has to be the switchboard. Let's hope it's nothing serious. I need some sleep."

As Lew disappeared into the other room, Ray put an arm around Gina's shoulders. "I'll bet you didn't know that Saturday is the last day of muskie season. Think you'd have time to join me in the boat? Get one more day on the water before it freezes over?"

Before Gina could answer, Lew charged into the room, pulling on her uniform jacket. Eyes dark with worry, she motioned to Osborne to grab his own coat. "It's Mildred Taggert. A trucker stopping by for cigarettes just found her unconscious in the parking lot. An ambulance is on its way. Doc, follow me."

"What about the girls? Are they okay?" said Osborne.

"Yes, according to neighbors at the scene. They may have been asleep before but they're certainly awake now."

"Well, Lew, if an ambulance is called is there really a need for you—"

"The guy who called 911 said she's bleeding badly from the head. He thinks she may have fallen and hit her head or who knows? She could have been robbed. Either way, I have to go."

"Right behind you," said Osborne.

"Me, too," said Ray. "Gina, I'll drop you off first."

"Are you kidding? You'll drop me off after we see what the story is."

FOURTEEN

As Osborne and Lew drove their cars into the parking lot behind Mildred's Food Shop, an SUV emblazoned with the insignia of the county sheriff pulled in behind and parked between Lew's cruiser and the ambulance from Saint Mary's Hospital. "We got your call for assistance, Chief Ferris," said a young deputy sheriff as he jumped from his car and ran towards Lew.

"Appreciate it. Not sure what we got here yet," Osborne heard her say as he opened his car door and reached into the backseat for the medical bag that he was now happy he'd forgotten to drop off at his house earlier.

Lit by the headlights from four vehicles plus the back porch lights of neighbors on both sides, the parking lot for Mildred's Food Shop and the old barn stood in relief against the November night. As he hurried to catch up with Lew, Osborne noticed that the wire cage in front of the barn looked different from earlier that day—now the door was wide open but the interior still empty.

Off to the left and close to the house lay Mildred Taggert: her body in its black tunic and loose black slacks sprawled sideways on the asphalt, her face a sliver of white. An EMT, crouched over the body, looked up as Osborne and Lew approached. He shook his head as he said, "No pulse, Dr. Osborne. Too late, I'm afraid. We got here within four minutes of the 911 call, too. Take a look," he said, pointing, "that is one nasty wound on the side of her head there."

Osborne knelt over the old woman. Her neck was arched, the head thrown back as if reeling from a blow. Her lovely, long silver hair, knocked from its trim knot, spread like mercury across the asphalt, gleaming in the light—as did the blood. The blood black and moving, trickling along ruts and across clumps of loose tar.

After taking a moment to pull on a pair of Nitrile gloves, Osborne leaned forward to gently tip Mildred's head to one side so that he and Lew, leaning over from behind him, could get a better look at what the EMT meant by "a nasty wound." Osborne looked up at her. "Right," she said in a grim tone as she nodded in agreement.

Mildred did not fall and hit her head nor was she bludgeoned. And it wouldn't take an AWOL coroner or a retired dentist to tell a woman who hunted what she was looking at: a single bullet—shot at close range—had done the job.

"You think that's an exit wound, Doc?" Lew twisted around, eyes scanning the house, the barn, the neighbors' yards. "I'm wondering from which direction she was shot."

"I'll have to defer to the pathologist on that," said Osborne. "Afraid I can't hazard a guess even. The best I can do is record a bullet to the head as apparent cause of death." Osborne pulled off the gloves. "Better send Ray home for his cameras before she's moved."

"Yep. Looks like we'll be here awhile, doesn't it? Are you okay with that, Doc? I can use your help with the girls. Find out what they heard or saw—the neighbors, too. Oh—and I'll need to find a place for the girls to stay." She gave a heavy sigh. "No sleep for the weary."

He answered with a rub of her shoulder. "I wonder if Mildred even knew what hit her…" he said, his voice trailing off as he stared down at the old woman. He wondered, too, if she had discovered the truth about Daisy. Had she suspected someone of stealing or killing her pet? One thing he knew for sure: Mildred would not have hesitated to confront the guilty party—and she would not have been nice.

"Lew—" Just as Osborne realized he better mention the dead animal, Ray came running up with Gina in tow.

"Oh, no—my poor friend," said Ray, his face falling. "Poor, poor Mildred. This—" he turned to Gina "—is so sad. Since I was six years old, I've been stopping by Mildred's shop almost every day. I've always bought my fishing licenses from her. She's an institution in Loon Lake." He pressed his fingers against his eyes, then took a deep breath. "I can't believe this is happening."

Lew patted his shoulder, her own eyes glistening. Osborne felt it, too. Sadness hovered like a silent prayer between the three of them. Each had known this woman in different ways and over many years. Mildred may have been gruff, she may have intimi- dated—but she was knit into the fabric of Loon Lake, into their daily lives.

Lew broke the silence. "Whoever it was used a gun."

"Yeah, I thought that might be the case," said Ray, his eyes raking the parking lot and what could be seen of the barn and the house as if he expected the shooter to be watching them. "One of the neighbors over there by the driveway said he heard something about half an hour ago. Thought it was a backfire. Obviously not."

"How fast can you get out to your place and back with those cameras?" said Lew.

"Twenty, twenty-five minutes. I better bring lights, too. C'mon, Gina—let's go. I'll drop you by your place."

"What do you think, Chief?" said Gina. "Can I be of help here? I'm more than willing—"

A retching sound from the dark alley that ran along the south side of the barn caused them all to turn and peer into the shadows. Osborne could barely make out the figure of Frances Dark Sky, one arm against the building for support, vomiting.

"Oh, the poor kid," said Ray, his voice sounding as helpless as Osborne sensed they all felt. "That's Frances… "

"Gina," said Lew, "would you mind—see if you can help? See if one of the neighbors will let her sit down inside? I can't allow the girls into Mildred's house until we secure the crime scene."

Before she could finish, Gina had darted into the dark alley. She called out in a soft voice: "Frances? I'm Gina Palmer. I'm here with Chief Ferris and Dr. Osborne. Can I help you find somewhere to sit until you feel better? Okay?" But Frances shook her head and staggered farther down the alley.

"Stay with her," said Lew.

"I will. I can imagine how she's feeling. I'll stay close by until she's ready," said Gina. She watched Frances for a second then turned back towards the lighted parking lot. "Here," she said, throwing her car keys at Ray, "you take my car."

Ray grabbed for the keys but missed. He bent to pick them up, then dropped to his knees. His voice changed. "Chief Ferris—come here. Walk carefully." The sheriff's deputy started over but Ray waved him back. The deputy stopped but said, "If you need cameras and lights, I can have some rushed over."

"If it's okay with Chief Ferris, it's okay with me," said Ray, still poised over the keys. "Save us some time."

"Yes, by all means, whatever you guys can spare," said Lew.

"Chief, careful now—watch where you're stepping," said Ray as Lew approached. He pointed. Two brass casings from spent bullets lay on the ground. "Someone got sloppy with their ammunition—those are .223-caliber bullets. I've been seeing a lot of those around lately. They use 'em with black rifles."

"I don't like black rifles," said Lew.

"What are you two talking about?" asked Gina, listening but keeping an eye on Frances.

"Black rifle's a modified assault rifle that some hunters like for small game," said Ray. "It's got a scope that's good at close range."

"Ah," said Lew. She glanced around. "Whoever shot Mildred could have been waiting for her right here. Or—" she looked skyward "—up in the barn maybe?"

"Or dropped these as they ran down the alley towards the field back there," said Ray.

HALF AN HOUR LATER, with Ray busy shooting the photos necessary before Mildred's body could be moved, Osborne worked alongside Lew, taking notes as she questioned the neighbors living on both sides of the shop and who were now clustered nearby watching the proceedings. With the exception of the man who thought he'd heard a backfire, everyone else had been asleep or watching television and hadn't heard anything remarkable.

"My husband's right. It's those damn motorcycles," chimed in the woman whose husband thought he had heard backfire. They lived on the other side of Mildred's shop and their fence ran along the shop's parking area. "They pull into Mildred's all times of day and right up to closing time, too. They make s-o-o much noise with backfires and those loud pipes—I make it a point not to pay attention. I'd be mad all the time if I did. Can't tell you how many times I called city hall 'bout it, too."

"Y'know, that field back there behind the barn," said another woman a few minutes later after introducing herself as Margie Cook and inviting Gina and the Dark Sky sisters—along with Lew and Osborne—into her kitchen to stay warm, "kids are out there with BB guns so often, tell you the truth I don't pay much attention."

"What about you girls? Did you hear anything?" said Lew from where she stood near the refrigerator in the small kitchen.

Frances, who had let Gina persuade her to come inside, sat with both arms splayed across the table and slumped back into her chair, her eyes closed. She was so pale Osborne was worried she might faint.

She opened her mouth to answer Lew but Josie, sitting across from her sister, spoke up first. "We got dropped off around eight and both of us had school work so we went right to our rooms," she said. "Right, Frances? Mrs. Taggert always made us go to bed early Sunday nights. She didn't like how we would come home from the Reeces' pretty tired after the weekend. We have to get up at five-thirty to catch the bus for school, y'know. I'm right, Frances, right?"

Frances, eyes still closed, nodded in agreement and then said, "Yes, we got home just before eight. I was in my room here in the house getting ready for school. I heard a couple customers come in but Mrs. Taggert was in the shop and I had the TV on watching Masterpiece Theatre for extra credit in my English class. I didn't hear anything until that siren…" The girl's voice cracked with a sob. Gina, sitting beside her, slid a glass of water her way. Every few minutes she would press a cool, wet cloth against the girl's forehead, which Frances did not resist.

"I'm worried she's in shock," Gina had whispered to Osborne and Lew when they first walked into the warm, well-lit kitchen. But Frances had refused to lie down. She insisted on being at the table.

Josie, with bright eyes and a face that bordered on cute was two years younger and the opposite of her sister. Where Frances was lanky and awkward, her features cramped in a lopsided grimace, Josie was built much lower to the ground and so compact she reminded Osborne of a raccoon—but maybe that was because he still had Daisy on his mind.

Her face was broad across the cheekbones and her skull more rounded with features softer, more symmetrical than her sister's. While Frances seemed half dazed, Josie was alert, eyes darting from Lew to Frances to Gina, then Osborne and back to Lew. Every few seconds, she sipped from a cup of hot chocolate, which she grasped in both hands. Tiny dark hands.

"Josie, you're so calm," said Lew after a few minutes. "This has been a hard day for you and Frances—first the tragedy for the Reece family and now this? Are you sure you're all right? You know, being too calm can be a symptom of shock, too."

Josie, surprised by the question, straightened up in her chair and mustered a half-smile. "But what good would it do for me to like, totally lose it? I'm sorry Mrs. Taggert is…someone has to take care of me and Frances—" she glanced over at her sister "—and I don't think right now that someone is Frances."

Lew gave her a long, searching look before saying, "I understand your mother is back on the reservation…"

"So?" The tone in Josie's voice was challenging. "I'm not going back there."

Frances sat up and stared at her sister. "You didn't tell me…"

"I only heard yesterday from Mrs. Reece. Mildred told her," said Josie, her voice escalating in defense.

"Well," said Lew. "How would you feel about calling her? You girls need a place to stay. I can talk to her probation officer and see if he feels that would be appropriate." Frances shifted in her chair and the color started to come back into her face. She reached for the glass of water.

"Not an option," said Josie, her face tightening. "Anyway, I've already called our sister."

"Your sister?" said Lew. "You girls have another sister?"

"Blue— I called Blue. She's on her way over to get us. She said there's room for us to stay with her and Andy at the Murphys' house." As she spoke, her eyes glittered under the kitchen lights. It struck Osborne that the girl had the eyes of an animal, too. And something else. Raccoons are fierce when confronted. They don't back down.

"Chief Ferris," said Osborne, thinking it wise to change the subject, "do you mind if I ask the girls a few questions for the death certificate?" He opened the file folder of documents and stared down at the blank lines on the top page. "I'll do my best to take care of a few details here as quickly as possible."

"Please," said Lew, "I'll check on the status of things outside. The sheriff's department said they would send over another deputy…" She was out the door before she had finished her sentence.

"Okay, girls," said Osborne. "I need Mrs. Taggert's age, date of last birthday, immediate survivors besides yourselves. Close relatives…" The blank looks he got told him it would be fruitless to ask for much more than confirmation of Mildred's name, address and phone number.

"I know she has a will," said Frances, looking a little stronger but talking in a soft, hesitant voice. "And she uses this one accountant for the taxes—his name is in the file cabinet by the cash register."

Josie looked at her sister with a stunned expression. "How do you know all that?"

Frances averted her eyes and shifted her shoulders. "She had me doing the bookkeeping is all." Josie continued to stare at her sister.

"Oh, yeah, well how come—"

"How come what?" said Frances, her voice strong. Osborne hadn't raised two daughters not to know when tempers were on edge.

"Girls, look, let's drop this for now—we'll deal with this first thing in the morning. Frances, I'll arrange with Chief Ferris for you to have access to the file cabinet and any documents—"

But Frances was looking past him, through the kitchen window. She jumped to her feet and bolted out the door. A quick look through the window showed Osborne that the EMTs were about to lift Mildred's body onto sheets they had laid across a stretcher. Frances was running towards them.

"Gina, we better see what we can do to help," said Osborne as he hurried from the kitchen.

"Wait! You can't go there," cried Lew as Frances pushed past the EMTs.

Too late. The girl threw herself onto her knees beside the body of the old woman and, fingers caress-

ing the silver hair, she murmured in a voice so low that
Osborne and Lew could barely make out her words:
"I'll take care of things. I'll find Daisy for you. I'll run
the shop like you showed me. And whoever did this—
they'll pay. I'll make them pay."

Before she could say more, Lew grasped the girl by
the shoulders and pulled her to her feet. "Let's go,
Frances," she said, her voice kind but firm. "You and
Josie come with me into the house so we can get you an
overnight bag. I expect Blue will be here any moment."

FIFTEEN

IT WAS NEARLY TWO A.M. before Osborne got to bed. The house was quiet, Mike lightly snoring and Osborne staring at the ceiling. He thought of everything left undone: Mildred's death certificate and an extensive search of her house, the shop and the old barn. And that was only the beginning.

Nor was it his list. It belonged to Loon Lake Chief of Police Lewellyn Ferris. Standing near her cruiser with a rueful smile, she had first apologized for ruining his holiday. "I'll make it up to you," she'd said. "Ralph Steadman called yesterday and invited me to go fly fishing in Jackson Hole next June—it's an invitation for two. He's owed a freebie from an outfitter there. All we have to pay is transportation there and back."

"Whoa," said Osborne, "that sounds too good to be true."

Lew gave a happy shrug. "Give it a thought, Doc."

IT WAS RALPH'S SPORTING GOODS that had connected Osborne with Lew two years earlier when Osborne had asked Ralph to recommend a fly fishing instructor. Ralph, the instrument of good fortune at that time, had turned out to be of questionable value since. Though married, he was often seen with ladies other than his spouse in expensive restaurants in Boulder Junction and Eagle River. Not likely venues for selling lures, minnows or trout flies. And Osborne was well aware that Lew got more than a passing glance and a bonus trout fly from the guy. But while she might laugh off Ralph's flirtatious ways, guys know guys. Osborne would not miss that fishing trip.

"I'LL HAVE TO CHECK the calendar," he'd said in a lame voice, knowing full well every day for the rest of his life was available.

"Yeah, you do that, Doc," said Lew with that funny smile of hers. She knew she had him hooked. Her eyes turned serious then and she urged him to head home for some sleep in spite of what was left undone. "I'm planning on you helping out tomorrow, too, if that's okay. Either that or I'll have to have a panic attack," she said with a laugh before kissing him goodnight.

"With that list of yours, we should be in the office by four, five a.m. at the latest, don't you think?"

"Oh, not that early," she punched him in the arm. "See you at seven." Her laughter and the unexpected invitation got him all the way home with a light heart.

HE SCRUNCHED THE pillow under his right ear, then under his left, then back again. He lay on his back, staring up. He told himself that if he didn't sleep, rest alone would be good. He decided to let his mind drift to where he had hoped to be: in Lewellyn Ferris's double bed, the old brass bedstead with the quilt her grandmother had made and the crisp sheets under which she loved to sleep naked. Even when he was there. A nice thought…but it didn't lead to sleep.

He gave up. He put on a pot of coffee, let Mike out onto the frost-covered grass in the backyard and pulled his winter parka on over his thermal long underwear. Pouring a mug of coffee before the pot had finished filling, he made a mess on the hot plate and dabbed at it with paper towels.

The stone stairs that led down to his dock were glazed with ice, forcing him to hold on to the banister with one hand. A mist had fallen and November seemed ready at last to let winter in. Though it was hours before dawn, the sky was suffused with a glow from the moon wherever it was hidden. Standing on the dock and gazing around, he felt he was looking into heaven—the lake brimming with a dove-gray cumulus bordered in blue. The surface was still: iridescent, deep and serene. The water had seduced the sky.

He heard a swish and looked down. He saw a face and hands. A person swimming up from beneath the opaque surface but unable to push through. Water sprayed and a huge northern pike leapt at him, shivered in the icy air and fell back. Dead.

HE WOKE TO A soft snore from the dog. It took a full minute to convince himself that he was under his own blankets, in his own home, safe.

SIXTEEN

OSBORNE ARRIVED AT McDonald's shortly after six a.m. Only two of his regular coffee buddies were waiting in the usual booth.

"These November mornings are too darn chilly, way too easy to sleep in," said Herb Anderson, retired mill manager and Osborne's former duck hunting partner. Always a long, lanky man, Herb struck Osborne as growing thinner and longer with age. Every time he saw the skinny guy he would remember sitting in freezing duck blinds, fingers clutching a thermos for warmth. That was one sport he sure as hell didn't miss.

"Yep," said buddy number two, Jim Craigemeier, "we're the diehards. We're the crazy ones, doncha know." Jim, more rotund than he should be, completely bald and widowed like Osborne, had recently retired from the accounting firm, now run by his sons, that he had started right around the time Osborne opened his dental practice. With offices across the street from one another—and Jim's located above Marty's Bar—the two men had shared way too many end-of-work-day brewskis.

"Morning, Jim," said Osborne, sliding into the

booth with a large coffee in hand. "Say, didn't you used to do tax returns for Mildred Taggert?"

"Still do. She's one of thirty clients I've held on to. Been doin' their taxes for years and Milly's one of 'em. Why?"

Osborne shared the details of the night before and when he was finished the two men stared at him, mouths open. "Mildred Taggert?" Herb blinked. "That woman kept a shotgun under her cash register. No way she got robbed—unless someone jumped her. Mildred didn't trust anyone, you know that. How the hell—"

"Well, it happened," said Osborne. "What mystifies me is the fact she was shot and no one heard gunfire," said Osborne. "One neighbor thought he heard a backfire is all. How does that happen? In city limits, no less."

"You know what, Doc," said Jim, pausing to rip the edge off a packet of sugar and dump it into his coffee, "I'll tell ya exactly how it happens." He shook his right index finger at Osborne. "I would bet you every weekend I hear what sound like gunshots—but they're these damn kids shootin' off fireworks.

"You know my place up on the river there. We have city streets, city water. I'm not out in the country. And we've got all that noise. Take a look around—see all the fireworks stands we got now? They're everywhere! Year 'round. Used to be you only saw 'em Fourth of July. Most of what they sell is illegal—I think. But that doesn't stop anyone. Hell, some kids in my neighborhood were shooting 'em off last night. Thanksgiving, for crissake."

Herb, shaking his head, said, "Now who would pick on poor old Mildred? An old woman for heaven's sake."

"And they shot her pet raccoon," said Osborne. "It wasn't until I mentioned that to Chief Ferris that it occurred to me that killing her pet might have been a warning to Mildred. Who knows? Maybe that was just a coincidence and not the same person… Likely not, now that I think about it. Not the same gun anyway. Looked to me like a .22-caliber pistol was used on the animal. Ray found a couple bullets dropped, we think, by the person pulling the robbery—.233-caliber."

"Oh, jeez," said Herb. "One of those black rifles. My son-in-law has one of those."

"I doubt your son-in-law was lurking in Mildred's parking lot last night."

"Of course not, but a lotta the guys he hunts with got those guns."

The three men sat silent over their tall paper cups of hot coffee, mulling the bad news.

"So, Jim," said Osborne after a few sips, "would you happen to know if Mildred kept much cash in the store?"

Jim took a swig of his coffee. "Always looked to me like she kept a cash drawer with no more than what she needed. Years in the business taught her that. She made deposits twice a week. I know because when it came time to do her taxes, the books she kept were meticulous. You don't know what a pleasure it is to do that woman's taxes."

"Spoken as a true accountant," said Herb with a chortle. "Who the hell else does taxes for fun?" Jim gave him the dim eye.

"Any idea who her lawyer might be?" said Osborne, anxious to cross one item off Lew's list.

"No lawyer that I know of, why?"

"Well, I need more information for the death certificate than the Dark Sky sisters have been able to tell me so far."

"Why didn't you say so right away, Doc? I've got everything you need."

Osborne gave Jim a startled look. "You do? How's that?"

"Guess I've been the closest thing she's ever had to a business manager. Between the two of us, we kept all her deeds and tax records in a safety deposit box and I have one of the two keys. She wanted me to have it. Just in case, y'know."

"Do you know if there's information in there on relatives we need to contact?"

"That old lady was married once many years ago. No children. Divorced the guy. Don't know his name—she mentioned him only once as 'that sonofabitch.' You know Mildred turned ninety-three this year."

"Jim, I know nothing. Is there any legal reason I shouldn't get this documentation from you? Those poor girls—"

"Whoa, hold on, my friend. Those 'poor' girls are not so poor. At least one isn't."

Osborne studied his friend's face. He thought of Daisy and of Mildred's collection of stuffed raccoons, of Josie and her tiny little hands. "Let me guess, she left her estate to the young one—Josie."

"Now what makes you think that?"

"Because she's a charmer."

"That may be true, but Mildred told me she was lazy. She had me witness a new will for her last spring. Divided her estate in two: half goes to Frances Dark Sky, the other half to an animal rescue shelter. Not a penny for Miss Josie."

"How much money are we talking about?" said Herb. "I recall Mildred buying some land from the mill years back. Likely that's worth a pretty penny."

"She owned land here and in Rhinelander that she did real well with," said Jim. "You could learn a lot from old Mildred if you just paid attention. She sold a couple parcels to Wal-Mart, some to Home Depot. Doc, that land was tag alder swamp when you and I first moved here. But Mildred was canny—had a real eye for spotting traffic patterns. Always thinking ahead. Yep. One smart lady." Jim nodded his head in approval, then sipped from his coffee.

"Jim," said Osborne, "just answer Herb's question—how much?"

"I'd say Miss Frances Dark Sky woke up this morning worth something close to a million maybe."

"Holy cow," said Herb.

Osborne was stunned. "Do you think those girls had any idea how much their foster mother was worth?" said Osborne.

"I doubt it," said Jim. "Far as I'm aware, Mildred and myself are the only parties who knew her net worth. She never used a banker, even when she bought property. Paid cash. She made me sign an agreement I would never discuss her finances unless she died or gave me permission.

"You know, Doc, there is something funny about all this. Mildred called me last week. She asked if I had my key for the safety deposit box and would I mind putting a letter in the box for her. Her arthritis had gotten so bad she didn't like leaving the shop. So I took care of that for her."

"Did you read the letter?"

"No, I did not. Never did anything she didn't ask me to. But she did say she was keeping a copy in the shop somewhere as well."

SEVENTEEN

Lew was on the phone when Osborne walked into her office. Even though it was early—only seven-thirty—the papers strewn across her desk made it obvious she had been in for at least an hour already.

"Very good, Miriam," Lew was saying as she glanced up at Osborne, "I appreciate your cooperation. Tomorrow then. Ten a.m. at your home." She hung up, rolled her chair back and slapped both hands on top of the papers in front of her. "Doc, making headway here. That was Miriam Murphy, mother of Blue's fiancé. The family is catching a flight this evening and will be ready to meet with us in the morning. Do you mind joining me for that last round of questioning the party guests?"

"Not in the least. I know the Murphys but not well. On a few occasions when they had a dental emergency they would call and I'd patch 'em up until they could get back to their regular dentist. If I recall correctly, the husband is quite a bit older than his wife."

"Like you and me," grinned Lew.

"No-o-o," said Osborne, going along with the tease. "Like I would guess a twenty to twenty-five year age difference. George was in his sixties when that boy was born."

"How do you know all this?"

"Mary Lee and her friends. They were always intrigued with the rich folk from down south, including Nolan's parents and certainly Nolan herself. Up until she was in her late teens, she would stay at her grandfather's for a month or so every summer. He let her join the water-ski club one year and rumors flew that she might marry a local boy. I always got that gossip as romance among the wealthy summer people was the favorite topic for discussion among the regulars at Mary Lee's bridge table. That and conniving to have their daughters meet the young men who were heirs to all that Chicago money."

"Ah," said Lew.

"Speaking of age differences, that reminds me, Lewellyn—if my old roommate and his wife who've been parked in my house for six excruciating weeks hadn't decided to move out yesterday, I was planning to call on you for help."

"What—hand them an eviction notice?" Lew asked the question even as she was already sorting through the pages of her notepad and had her hand on the phone ready to make the next call.

"Not exactly. I was planning to tell them they had to move out because you were moving in."

Lew took her hand off the phone. "Oh, I was—was I?"

"Yes, for at least twenty years—which would preclude their being able to park their stuff in my garage. We would need the storage."

Lew gave him a long look with laughter in her eyes. "But they moved out."

"Yes, they did. But that doesn't mean they won't be back. Furnace might not work in the cabin they're renting, doncha know."

"Good try, Doc. I appreciate the thought."

"I know—but now I can tell my daughters I tried. Right?"

"You can tell them that and you can tell them I'm treating you to a fish fry tonight because you are working one long Friday—don't take that jacket off."

BUD OLENTOWSKI, Nolan's stockbroker who, with his wife, had been at the Reeces' party, had offices just three blocks from the Loon Lake Police Department headquarters. A brisk walk on the cold November day. "Brrr!" said Lew as they hurried along. "The lakes have to freeze over with weather like this. It's so late not to have ice yet."

"Loon Lake is still open," said Osborne. "First Thanksgiving I remember with open water." As he opened the door to the brokerage firm, he said, "So we're seeing Bud—"

"Bud and his wife, Linda. She agreed to meet with us here as well."

The couple was waiting for them in Bud's office. Bud, a heavy-set, genial man with florid features thanks to an appetite for red meat and neat scotch, had inherited a business built by his father and grandfather. His wife, Linda, who was in her early sixties, had been in Mary Lee's garden club. As gracious as her husband

was genial, she was alarmingly thin. Osborne remembered as he walked into the room that she had had a
recent brush with cancer.

"We were stunned to get your call yesterday," said
Linda, getting to her feet to shake hands. She was
dressed in a simple black pants suit and an ivory shirt,
her short hair tucked behind her ears and no make-up
that Osborne could see. "I can't imagine this happening to Nolan."

"An absolute shock," said Bud as they all sat down.
The Olentowskis had listened intently as Lew sketched
in what was known and what she hoped to hear from
them. It was Bud who answered first. "We were there
for dinner from a little after six and stayed until around
ten fifteen or so. Is that right, Linda?"

"Yes. And Nolan had planned a lovely evening to
celebrate Blue's engagement. Just family and close
friends—you've mentioned everyone who was there—
both families, including those darling Indian girls that
Nolan dotes on. Then us and the Pokornys."

"And the catering staff," added Osborne.

"Yes," said Linda.

"No one else?" said Lew.

The husband and wife stared at each other, thinking.
"Someone must have dropped the girls off. It wasn't
Blue because she was late for some reason. I remember
Nolan getting irritated over that... But whoever their
ride was didn't stay," said Linda.

And so the conversation went with Lew asking
questions about the evening and Osborne taking
notes. Both Linda and Bud agreed that Nolan and her

husband seemed relaxed as the evening progressed with no noticeable incidents beyond the spilling of a glass of wine.

"And Frances and Josie were there the entire evening?" said Lew.

"Yes, though Nolan had arranged for them to watch a movie after dinner—down in the family room—so they didn't have to be bored by us grown ups.

"They're Nolan's pets, you see," said Linda. "She discovered the girls last year and made a big deal about how she wanted to include them in the family and see that they had opportunities—like, you know, education, nice clothes—have a better sense of what they might achieve in life. I thought it rather an odd arrangement myself that they would live at that teeny little shop during the week but spend the weekend at the Reeces' mansion. Quite an economic disparity if you know what I mean."

"Now, Linda," her husband cautioned, "the difference was not that extreme. The girls are getting a good education in the Loon Lake school system and it made no sense to change their routines until the adoptions went through."

"Oh?" said Lew. "I haven't heard that they were going to be adopted."

"Bud…" It was Linda's turn to caution. "My husband doesn't know all the details. Initially Nolan had planned to adopt both girls but just recently she'd begun to question if she could handle both. Little Josie is a cutie and gets along with everyone, but that Frances—well, Nolan and I had discussed that she might need counseling."

"She needs counseling?!" Bud exploded. "I'd say Nolan Reece is the one needing counseling."

"Now, Bud," said Linda, in a chastising tone. "Ignore him. Nolan could be frustrating. Back to Frances—it was just that no matter what Nolan did for her, she couldn't get the girl to open up. Very introverted young woman. We thought something in her childhood maybe…"

Lew turned to Bud and said, "Off the subject of the guests that evening and moving on here—am I to understand that Nolan Reece was worth over a billion dollars?"

"Oh, gosh, no," said Bud, "who the heck said that? For a time she was a very wealthy woman but no, not that much. After the family firm was sold, I'd say sixty million at the most."

"A very successful businesswoman from the sound of it," said Lew. "Sixty million dollars is a lot of money."

"Was a lot of money," said Bud sitting up and pulling his chair forward. "This requires some explaining. Nolan's grandfather was one of the lumber barons of the early 1900s. When he died, his son, her father, took over and sold off most of the forestland, diversifying the family fortune. He got into drugstores—built a huge chain of drugstores. And he ran that company until the day he died of a heart attack at his desk. So Nolan's family has owned the lake property up here since her grandfather's day. It was after her father died that Nolan tore down the original estate to build that beautiful home you see today. Quite a place, isn't it?"

"Her mother had died years earlier," added Linda, "so Nolan inherited everything."

"This was about eight years ago," said Bud. "Nolan thought she could take over and run this financial conglomerate that her father had managed so well even though she had no training, no experience and, trust me, no people skills."

"Careful, Bud, you don't want to imply she was a bad person."

"She was a bad manager," said Bud, ignoring his wife. "She was awful. Her father had hired very bright guys over the years, lieutenants he could trust to run their divisions without his micromanaging. But Nolan never understood the value of listening to those people, of trusting them to make good decisions. I don't know whose advice she took but it was bad. Within a year, good people were fleeing that organization in droves.

"All that saved her was that the old man had never taken it public, so when the revenues tanked she didn't have shareholders to battle. At least she was smart enough to know things were going downhill, so when an offer, a good offer, came out of the blue—she took it. Sold the company lock, stock and barrel."

"She had no people skills, you say." Lew tapped her pen thoughtfully on her notepad.

"She could be a lovely person, but volatile," said Bud. "Your best friend one minute and outraged over some small thing the next. And bullheaded. Once she made her mind up, she never backed down. It was her way or the highway."

"But once you know her, you understand that—and she's been known to apologize," said Linda.

"You two appear to have gotten along with her," said Lew.

"She was, for a while, my biggest account," said Bud. "I'm not going to lie to you. I have had to work for every penny. Linda knows that." He shot his wife a quick glance. "I had stressful days with Nolan but I sure as hell didn't have reason to hurt the woman. She hurt herself plenty already."

"What do you mean by that?" said Lew.

"I mean she took bad advice. Two years ago, right after sinking a ton of money into that house, she invested every remaining penny she had in a hedge fund run by some numbnut in Lake Forest. It tanked big time nine months ago."

"Are you saying she lost sixty million dollars?"

"Yep. The woman went broke. Well, maybe not broke by our standards—she had a couple hundred thousand in bonds still, which she had me to thank for. The property is mortgaged to the hilt, too. But the sixty million? Vaporized." There was silence in the office.

Linda's voice was soft as she asked, "Is there any possibility this was a suicide?"

"Afraid not," said Lew. She turned toward Osborne. "Doc, anything you want to ask here?"

"Just one thing," said Osborne. "Were either of you aware of anyone leaving the party early? Aside from the girls watching a movie in the family room?"

"You know, it was one of those evenings where you all go along having a pleasant time," said Linda, "then someone looks at their watch and it's later than you think. So, with the exception of Blue and Barry who were standing with Andy waving goodnight to all of us, I think we all left together."

"Did you think it was odd that Nolan wasn't there?" said Osborne.

"Not really," said Linda, "she'd had quite a bit to drink. She was starting to slur her words. We thought she went up to her bedroom and passed out."

"This is very helpful," said Lew. "I want to thank you both for your time. And I'm very likely to have to call you again with more questions."

"Please," said Bud as he and Linda got to their feet, "don't hesitate. Even though Nolan could be difficult, we considered her a dear friend. Like family, y'know, they're kinda wacky and some days you love 'em to death—while other days you could kill the suckers."

At the stricken look on his wife's face, he shut up.

EIGHTEEN

"I STILL DON'T believe it. When Vern told me about it last night—I was sure someone had it all wrong! Nolan Reece dead? Un-n-n-believable."

Marge Pokorny had rushed to her husband's law office within minutes of taking his phone call in her office at the Loon Lake High School where she was a guidance counselor. After arriving—though encouraged to join Lew and Osborne and take one of the chairs in front of her husband's desk—she ignored the request, choosing instead to pace back and forth at the back of the room, arms flailing.

"You're telling me there was a murderer somewhere close to their house that night? While we were there? Stalking us?" she said, pointing at her chest. Raking her short black hair back with both hands, she turned to her husband, eyes wide with disbelief. "How can this be happening?"

Lew threw Osborne a glance: she had only so much time for drama queens.

Osborne winked. He knew the drill.

"Mrs. Pokorny," he said, his voice low and calm— a tone he had found worked wonders to disarm the hysteria of patients terrified at the thought of the

dentist's drill—"you and your husband are key wit-
nesses. Whatever you tell us will be of great value to
the investigation and the sooner we can get started,
the sooner Chief Ferris will be able to resolve this
very serious situation. People are at risk and we need
your help…"

OSBORNE KNEW THE POKORNYS from a distance as they
also attended St. Mary's early morning Mass on
Sundays. Of medium height, Vern was a nice-looking
man in his mid-forties with straight black hair, a mous-
tache and a pleasant, easy-going manner. His wife was
wound pretty tight—obvious from the way she would
cuff her children if they fooled around during Mass.
Dark-haired like her husband, Marge was short and
wiry with intense dark eyes under the bangs outlining
her heart-shaped face.

Vern had been at the sheriff's department late in the
evening on Thanksgiving Day assisting a client, another
lawyer (who had just been arrested for his fourth DWI),
when he'd heard the news of Nolan's death mentioned
on the scanner. He had called the switchboard immediately to leave a message that not only was he Nolan's
local legal counsel but that he and his wife had been at
the engagement party the night before.

Lew had returned his call early that morning, assur-
ing Vern that he was already on her list of people she
needed to question. Given that his law office was just
two blocks down from Bud Olentowski's, it was agreed
that she and Osborne come by right after the earlier
meeting. Like Bud, he had arranged for his wife to sit in.

"DR. OSBORNE'S RIGHT, Margie, hon," said Vern. "Now would you sit down, please?"

"I'm sorry if I'm upset," said Marge with a huff, "not like things like this happen everyday." But she did as she was asked, then crossed her legs and started pumping her right foot up and down, up and down.

"So, Vern, Marge, you were at the Reeces' from when to when exactly?" Lew asked.

"I would say we arrived around six thirty and left just after ten with everyone else," said Vern.

Lew proceeded with a series of questions similar to the ones she had asked the Olentowskis. Vern and Marge had little to add to the events of the evening. They, too, had noticed that Nolan had had a lot to drink and hadn't found it unusual that she retired—or so they thought—before the evening was over.

"Vern," said Osborne, "as I was trying to complete the death certificate, Andy Reece said he was unsure of some of Nolan's personal information and that you might be better able to answer. He wasn't sure of her date of birth and he wasn't sure which address to list as her permanent residence. May I say I find it a little odd that he would not know these things?"

"Certainly, I'll do my best to fill in the blanks. In case you haven't guessed, Andy and Nolan's marriage has been…let's say 'platonic'…for years, with Andy out of the loop of her personal affairs for quite some time now. He called here this morning and told me I have his approval to share whatever information you might need. Nolan regularly lied about her age—that's why he was uncertain. And I think you should use the Loon Lake address as her permanent residence. She's been living up here full time since the house was finished."

"Close relatives aside from her daughter and her husband?"

"None. Her mother died years ago and her father passed away eight years ago. No siblings. In fact—" Vern paused to open a thick folder resting in front of him "—Andy thought it might help if we take a look through a copy of the will. I'll be dropping a copy off with the family later today as well.

"You'll see the will is straightforward and includes the covenants of two trusts established by Nolan's father, Norman Marsdon—one benefits Nolan, the other her daughter, Blue, who is referred to throughout as 'Eleanor.'"

Vern flipped through several pages then said, "The official document is in the family safe deposit box down in Illinois but Nolan had me keep a copy here for reference back when she was selling the family firm. She had the right to sell the company and all related assets in her trust—but not the other. Her father was determined to protect some assets for his granddaughter. It's as if he knew his daughter lacked good judgment when it came to business decisions."

"What about Andy Reece?"

"He receives what remains in Nolan's trust, which was not Nolan's wish per se but state law." Vern paused. "I understand you've spoken with Bud and you know the woman lost millions of dollars. Andy stands to inherit about two hundred thousand is all.

What you may find interesting is the twenty million dollars that's in the trust for Eleanor aka Blue."

"Even though Nolan had control over that trust?"

"She couldn't touch it."

"But I thought—" said Osborne. "We were told by someone who knows the family that she had heard that Blue would be disinherited if she didn't marry the man her mother wanted her to marry."

"Typical Nolan—always bullshitting. Working with her over the years, I cannot tell you how easy it was for that woman to lie. She did it on purpose—to get her way, to intimidate people. So she couldn't touch the trust or change the terms but she did have one small lever of control. One condition of the trust was to be kept secret—the simple fact that Nolan had no control over it.

"She convinced her father that Blue was in need of strict parental discipline and that implying that Nolan could change the trust would help her guide her daughter through adolescence. Since Nolan had been a nightmare of a teenager herself, he agreed to that. Given that she's now dead, I have the legal right to tell that young woman the truth."

"So Nolan Reece lied to her daughter in hopes of forcing this marriage?" said Lew.

"It appears that way."

"Vern, you can't be telling us that you let this happen?" said Marge, foot pumping even faster.

"I had to. If I had opened my mouth, trust me, Nolan would have sued the bejesus out of us, Marge. Frankly, that family is so screwed up I'm not sure what good telling Blue the truth would have done. Given her behavior these past last few years, I think her mother was wise to keep that from her. It appears it was the only measure of control she had over the kid."

"May I add a few comments of my own?" said Marge. Osborne and Lew shifted their chairs to face her. "I realize my husband, the lawyer, is an expert on these issues, but as a guidance counselor with a Masters in psych, I'm not stupid when it comes to people."

"I doubt you are," said Lew, encouraging her to continue. "I'm quite interested in your observations, Marge."

"On the numerous occasions that Vern and I have been guests in the Reece home, I have always been struck by how angry Nolan is—was, I mean. An anger simmering just below the surface. You never knew what might set her off. The most innocent remark could do it. And she was always watching, always."

"C'mon, Marge, she wasn't always angry," said Vern. "She seemed quite happy and gracious the other night—"

Marge threw her hands up in the air. "Go right ahead and disagree with me, Vern, but I sensed it every time I was around her. Maybe women are better at picking up on that. I don't know. Let me put it this way—she wasn't someone I would want to be around if I didn't have to—she made me damn nervous."

"A lot of people make you nervous, Marge honey," said Vern, rocking back in his chair.

"Don't 'Marge honey' me, Vern. I'm a professional, I know what I'm saying."

"Okay, okay," said Vern, tossing the pen he'd been toying with into the air.

"If you disliked her so much, why did you spend time with her?" said Lew.

"She's Vern's client."

"I did work for her father and I'm cheaper than the Chicago guys," said Vern.

"Even though she had lost so much money, she had legal obligations that had to be met. We were in the process of rescinding a major donation that she had promised—and there are a few other promises she couldn't keep."

"Such as?" said Lew.

"Oh, the tough one is she promised so much to the Dark Sky sisters. She said she would pay for their education and I know she told Josie that she would be an heiress some day. She adored that girl. Someone is going to be very disappointed, I'm afraid."

"Maybe Blue will step in, since she's certainly going to be in a position to do so," said Osborne. Blue had struck him as a serious, thoughtful young woman. If she was bright and caring, why would she not at least cover the girls' college costs?

"I don't know about that," said Vern. "Certainly something to be discussed. Nolan had a bad habit of criticizing Blue in front of the sisters. Blue could have some mixed feelings about those girls. We'll have to see."

"Told you," said Marge. "She was not a happy person and she did her best to pollute the people around her. Now I know my husband thinks I'm overstating the case here but—" she gave Lew and Osborne a beseeching look "—you know what I mean? A person like that can have a lot of enemies."

OUTSIDE THE OFFICE, Osborne turned to Lew as they headed back towards the old courthouse and Lew's office. "Aren't the Pokornys a fun couple?"

Lew laughed. "I'm interested in that remark of Vern's—when he said Nolan had been a nightmare as a teenager. You know, it's not inconceivable that someone out of her past—"

"How about someone in her recent past," said Osborne. "Say a carpenter, a plumber or one of the subcontractors working on that house. Someone she refused to pay or verbally abused. Remember, Erin said she was very rude to the butcher at the Loon Lake Market. Who knows? Given what we're hearing, could be a long list."

NINETEEN

As Lew's cruiser wound its way up the drive to the Reece home, Osborne spotted a forest green Dodge Ram pick-up parked behind one of the Reeces' gray Range Rovers. "Isn't that the same truck that dropped off Frances and Josie yesterday?" he said, craning his head to look back as Lew pulled into an empty space between two familiar black vans parked in the spaces near the side door: the Wausau boys at work.

"Doug?" said Lew in surprise as she got out of the car and looked up to see a man, dressed in business clothes, standing in the doorway to the Reeces' kitchen. "I thought you retired." She ducked back into the car on the pretense of picking up files from the front seat but whispered to Osborne, "Don't you dare leave me alone with that man. He always stand too close and insists on telling dirty jokes."

"Who is he?" Osborne whispered back.

"Doug Jesperson."

"A good Scandinavian name."

"Yeah, well he's a creep. He was director of the Wausau Crime Lab. I thought he retired. He did retire. Wonder why the hell he's back now."

"Chief Lewellyn Ferris," said Jesperson, walking towards Lew with his arms open and a goofy smile on his face. A slight man with wispy dun-colored hair and pale skin, he was wearing a button-down shirt that did nothing to restrain the paunch drooping over the belt of his dark gray slacks. The lapels of his suit jacket held dustings of dandruff.

Lew ducked the open arms and backed away. "I thought you retired, Doug. What's the deal?"

"Holiday, kiddo. I fill in for the regulars on occasion. Good to see you. Had a word about an hour ago with your compatriot in the funny hat. Haven't seen him since."

"You mean Ray Pradt?"

"Yeah, boy, did he have a funny joke this morning. Did you hear the one about the milkman and the lady who ordered twenty-five gallons of milk for her bath?"

"Doug, I've got work to do. This is Dr. Paul Osborne—a deputy of mine. We need to sit down with the Reeces' ASAP. Switchboard said they've been allowed into the house. Do I assume you approved that?"

"So the milkman says, 'Twenty-five gallons! Don't you mean 2.5 gallons?'

"'No,' she says, 'I need it for my bath.'

"'Oh,' says the milkman, 'you need that pasteurized?'"

"Doug, put a lid on it," said Lew, brushing past him towards the door. "You know I don't like off-color jokes."

"It's a Ray joke."

"I don't listen to dirty jokes from him either." Lew

yanked open the door and disappeared into the house.

"So the lady says," Doug called after her, "'No, just up to my shoulders.' Get it? past—"

Osborne stopped in front of the guy and reached to shake his hand. "Nice to meet you, Doug. You're right. That is a Ray joke. I've heard it a few times. Good effort on the delivery."

A disheartened look on his face, Doug followed them into the Reeces' kitchen. "I asked the family to wait in the den," he said with a dismissive wave of one hand. "We needed some information from them as we processed the house, which, for the record, has yielded nothing of interest at this point. No evidence of forced entry, nothing missing. Three of us have been here since six this morning. I've got the team down in the boathouse right now. We may find more there. I'll let you know."

He gestured towards the closed door to the den and lowered his voice. "That guy in there—the victim's husband—a total freak. Got crap on that computer you wouldn't believe—"

"Porn?" asked Lew.

"Hell, no. Fantasy fishing. Guy's nuts about the stuff. And the daughter's not Miss Congeniality is she? You got your hands full with those two."

"You will take the computer and the cell phones with you—give me an analysis of the contents?"

"Of course, Lewellyn," he said in a tone so patronizing Osborne had the urge to remind him he was addressing a person carrying a gun. "I'll have techs work with them later today and once we got the data, we'll get back to you."

"Thank you," said Lew, ignoring his attitude. "One more thing, Doug—I called down to the lab after you had left this morning so I'm not sure if you got the message that Loon Lake had another homicide late last night—"

"The old lady who got robbed? Yeah, I got the message. Can't you handle that on your own? Get a detective over from the sheriff's department. Those guys need something to do." Doug picked up his coat and turned towards the door.

"But the shop," said Lew, "if she was assaulted indoors and forced from the building at gunpoint, Wausau has the technology to handle that evidence better than we do up here."

"Lewellyn, it's an old lady running a candy store. Maybe they got fifty bucks off her. Not like this situation."

"You mean the death of a prominent, wealthy individual merits a close look at the crime scene but the death of an elderly shopkeeper does not?"

"I didn't say that. I just don't think it's going to yield—"

"You don't think you're going to get interviewed on TV for investigating a robbery at Mildred's Food Shop—but you will be for looking into the death of the woman who was heir to one of the largest family fortunes in the Midwest, right?"

"Okay, okay, we'll head over there when we've finished here."

"You're sure? Because Loon Lake is happy to pay for the analysis of both these crime scenes. I—"

"I heard you," said Doug. He stormed out of the kitchen.

"No, Doug, wait," said Lew, running after him. "Something I want you to be sure to get when you're there."

"Don't tell me how to do my job, okay?"

"I have no intention of doing that. It's just that you should know that Mildred Taggert has been the foster mother to two teenage girls whose natural mother was just released from prison after serving time for dealing drugs on the reservation. I think it might be wise to check the girls' cell phones, too."

Jesperson made no attempt to hide his irritation as he gave a wave. "We'll take care of the details, Lewellyn."

Back in the kitchen, Lew stood with her hands on her hips staring down at the floor. After a few seconds, she looked up. "Doc, I don't think I handled that very well. Something about that man—just looking at him makes me mad."

"Well, Lew, I don't think you have to worry about whether he'll stop by Mildred's. I doubt he wants to be badgered by you for a while."

Lew's cell phone rang. She answered, spoke briefly and hung up. "The pathologist called. Nolan Reece died of blunt force trauma to the right side of her neck, which appears to have prompted a laryngospasm. No water in the lungs. They'll be analyzing the scrapings from under her nails and that may take until next Monday for results."

"What about all that scuffing we saw on her clothing?"

"No marks on corresponding areas of the body apparently. But I'll ask about that."

"WHO DRIVES THAT green pick-up I see in your driveway?" asked Lew after knocking, then opening the door to the den.

At the sound of Lew's voice, Blue uncurled her long, thin frame from the easy chair where she had been sitting with her feet up, arms hugging her knees. Scuffed, tight jeans and a close-fitting black T-shirt under a worn black leather jacket, her face devoid of makeup and her short hair tousled, she looked years younger than a twenty-something heir to millions. She looked like a teenager in need of a good night's sleep.

"That's Jake Cahak," she said. "He's the caretaker here. He's always around."

Andy rocked back in the swivel chair behind his desk and pushed himself to his feet. Given the rapid drop in temperature outdoors, Osborne was relieved to see he had traded the Bermuda shorts for a pair of dark brown corduroys and a navy blue sweater at least one size too big. He had bags under his eyes, visible beneath the dark rims of his glasses. He might have been crying.

"Jake Cahak," said Lew, "is that who dropped the girls off yesterday?"

"Oh, yes, Mother had arranged that, too—just like Thanksgiving dinner." The irony in Blue's voice was as unmistakable as the circles under her eyes. She, too, had been crying. Maybe Lew was wrong, thought

Osborne, and it's a Scandinavian trait to have delayed reactions.

"Jake takes care of all the upkeep this place needs," said Andy. "A good man—does anything you ask him to. He should be leaving in a few minutes. I asked him to pick up the dogs at the kennel. The Murphys don't have a dog so I didn't want ours running all over their place. And he'll pick up Frances and Josie on his way back—I thought they might be more comfortable over here now that we're allowed back in."

"What did he have to say about your wife's death?" said Lew.

"Pretty upset. Feels it's his fault an intruder got on the property. Yeah, he's promised to keep a very close eye on things."

"Folks," said Lew, "let's go into the kitchen where there's a little more room for all of us to talk—please?" Andy and Blue followed her out of the den and back into the kitchen.

"Since Frances and Josie were never allowed to drive that old heap of Mildred's, Nolan arranged for Jake to handle their transport on the weekends and whenever," said Andy as he pulled out a kitchen chair for Lew before sitting down himself. Blue took the chair beside Andy, giving him a pat of assurance on his shoulders as she did so.

"The night of the dinner party—would he have picked them up that night, too?" said Osborne. He glanced over at Lew. "The girls couldn't remember exactly what time they got home—he might know if he dropped them off."

"Good point," said Lew. She jotted down a note.

"Andy, how did you and your wife come to know the Dark Sky sisters? Through church or…how?"

"Fantasy fishing," said Andy. "It's my hobby—"

"Your obsession, you mean," said Blue, giving him a fond look.

"Well—" Andy hunched his shoulders in embarrassment "—I guess you can put it that way. That's why every day I liked to stop by Mildred's for the latest news. See, she posts the tournament bulletins on the wall behind the cash register, sells the fishing magazines I like, keeps a lunar calendar so you can see the major and minor fish feeding times."

"Perfectly innocent pastime," said Blue. "But you know what Mother did? Wait, Andy, you tell 'em what she did. It was unbelievable—but classic. Just classic." Blue rolled her eyes.

Osborne was surprised to hear Blue call Andy by his first name. Hadn't she called him "Dad" before? And she seemed so protective of the guy. Had something changed between the two?

"My wife thought I was having an affair—now, do you believe that? Me?" Andy pressed his right hand against his chest as he gave a sheepish grin. "So she followed me there one day and that's how she met the girls. Took a liking to little Josie right away."

"Oh, yes 'little Josie'—cute, perky—everything I'm not," said Blue. She cast a dim eye towards Lew and Osborne. "In case you can't tell, I'm tired of hearing about little Josie."

"And Frances?" said Osborne.

"Oh, Frances is okay," said Blue. "I like Frances.

She's a good egg, tries hard. Takes a lot of crap from that sister of hers, though. Frances I don't mind having around. A little bit of Josie goes a long way. But I'm talking too much—sorry, Andy."

"Nolan was ready for a new interest, something she could sink her teeth into—"

"Besides us," said Blue. "And a good thing, too. Andy and I? We were tired of being targets."

Ignoring Blue, Andy said, "The girls brought out the best in Nolan. I guess the way to put it is that Nolan always did better on her own than in a group— so the Dark Sky sisters became her special project. They needed a fairy godmother and Nolan could be that for them, expose them to a better way of life, help with their education, buy them nice clothes, fix up their rooms. See that they have things other kids have like iPods and laptops and—"

"And more clothes," said Blue. "My mother spent a thousand bucks on Josie's back-to-school stuff. A thousand bucks! Do you believe it?"

Andy played with the edge of a place mat on the table. "Nolan got so much enjoyment doing things for the girls that she decided to establish a foundation that would help more Native American girls."

"Yeah, well, Josie enjoyed the fact she promised to put her in her will," said Blue. She tapped her cigarette on the edge of a blue ceramic bluegill that doubled as an ashtray and said, "My mother had a habit of making promises she couldn't—or wouldn't— keep."

"Is that true, Andy?" asked Lew.

Andy was silent for a moment, then said, "My wife was not a well woman. Blue knows. We made allowances."

"I'd like to hear more about that," said Lew.

"From both of us together or individually?" said Blue. "If Andy doesn't mind, I'd rather we did it one on one or—" she glanced at Osborne "—two on one. I…well, I'll be more frank if I'm by myself. Andy, do you mind?"

"NOT IN THE least," said Andy, getting to his feet. Blue reached up for his hand, caught it and held on. "Are you okay?"

"I'm fine. Don't you worry about me," said Andy, patting her on the shoulder.

"I love you, man," said Blue with a squeeze of his hand before letting go. "Nothing's changed, you know."

"I know, sweetheart." He started towards the den, then stopped and turned back. "Chief Ferris? It's okay that I bought a new computer isn't it? I figured the crime lab might keep mine for a while and I really need to be online. I paid a guy at Best Buy to run one up from Wausau this morning and I have a receipt dated today. My fishing stats—we got a major bass tournament that I'm deep into…"

"I see no problem with new equipment," said Lew. She waited until Andy had shut the door to the den, and turned towards Blue.

But before she could get a word out, Blue sat straight up in her chair, leaned forward to stub out her cigarette, then reached into her pocket for the pack. As she tapped a fresh cigarette on the tabletop, she widened her eyes and with a sly grin said, "In case you haven't heard from other people and I'm sure you have—I am an alcoholic and a drug addict. I went into rehab at the age of thirteen and I have never gotten along with my mother. Just call me Suspect Number One."

With that she lit her cigarette, leaned back in her chair and chuckled. Osborne resisted chuckling along with her. Laconic, wry, funny: an odd girl. She might be nuts, she might be a killer—but he liked this girl.

TWENTY

"SOUNDS LIKE A CHALLENGING life," said Lew, her tone so offhand you would think everyone she knew was either a severe alcoholic or dedicated to controlled substances. "You plan to keep talking or do we ask questions?"

Osborne tucked his chin down so Blue couldn't see the amused expression on his face. Lew had a way of letting people know she was unfazed by outrageous behavior. It always had the desired effect: the bad actor found her blasé response so unsettling they were left speechless. Blue was no exception. Her grin vanished and her eyes darkened with thought.

"All right, I'll talk, but first I want to show you something," she said, getting to her feet. "We've been told it's okay to be in the house now, right?" Lew nodded. "So follow me upstairs."

The three of them went up the stairway in silence. The spacious upstairs hallway, like the rest of the house, was tastefully furnished with rustic furniture and wildlife paintings. A crimson Oriental runner protected the pegged wood floor. Blue motioned for them to follow her to the end of the hall where she opened a door. "This was my mother's suite," she said. "I was rarely allowed in here."

Lew and Osborne stepped into the unlit room behind her. Floor to ceiling drapes of a rich, cream-colored fabric were tied back to frame an expanse of glass overlooking the lake. Even though it was mid-afternoon, a combination of gray sky and cloud cover generated little light: the room was in shadows.

A pristine white coverlet was spread across the king-size bed with not a wrinkle in sight. Six matching pillows were lined up against the headboard—each angled the same degree and placed one overlapping another in identical spacing. Osborne wondered how long that took. Two étagères held a collection of paper-weights sandwiched between books and albums. Elegant mahogany dressers hinted at drawers filled with expensive garments.

The door to the bath stood open and Osborne followed Lew inside. The bath might have been a display in a high-end furniture store: its fixtures of tinted glass and stainless steel along with sets of snow-white towels appeared untouched by human hands. Artful arrangements of perfume bottles decorated the few shelves.

"Does anyone live here?" asked Lew. Osborne wondered the same—he saw no sign of everyday life.

"My mother. She was obsessive-compulsive. Everything had to be perfect. She made the housekeeper dust and vacuum this room twice a day, wash the bathroom floor daily and never, never move a book, a picture, anything. And one more thing…"

Blue strode across the bedroom to one of the étagères and reached for an album. As she turned towards Lew and Osborne, she flipped through the pages until she found what she was looking for. She turned a page, then another and held the open album out for them to see. A family photo of what had to be a young Nolan with her father and the woman likely to be her stepmother. The man's face had been cut out of the photo.

Blue turned the page to another photo of the same man with his arm held high to display a trophy northern pike—his face cut from the photo. Blue turned several pages and opened to a photo of a youthful Nolan standing beside a dark-haired man with horn-rimmed glasses. Nolan was cradling a baby in her arms so that both faced the camera. The child's face was cut out. On the same page was a photo of what appeared to be a christening: two parents and a baby with no face.

"And you want to know why I'm fucked up," said Blue with a wry laugh as she slammed the album shut and set it back on the shelf. "Those are the only pictures of me you will find in my mother's family albums. Lucky for me my grandfather took lots of pictures of me—or I would never have known I had a childhood."

BACK IN THE KITCHEN, they settled down to the table again. "Blue," said Lew, opening her notepad to a fresh page, "I'd like the name and phone number of your family's housekeeper. She may know if anything in the house has been disturbed or is missing."

"It's Mrs. Schultz," said Blue. "She took the week off to visit her family in Madison but I know she'll be back Sunday. She lives in Rhinelander and I think her husband's name is Albert."

"Thanks," said Lew, jotting the name down. "Now," she leveled her gaze at the young woman, "we've been told that you were late arriving for your engagement party and that your mother was upset by this. Tell us about that, would you please?"

"Do you mind if I smoke?"

"It's your house," said Lew. Blue pulled a lighter from the pocket of her jacket, tapped the end of one cigarette on a place mat and lit up. She inhaled, then blew smoke away from the table.

"I was at my weekly AA meeting over in Minocqua," said Blue. "Mother deliberately planned the party to conflict with my meeting so I deliberately planned to go anyway. I have a neighbor who goes, too. A young guy, lives up the road from here. We drive over and back together. Once a week, sometimes more often. Depends." Blue hesitated as worry crossed her face. "I said too much—I don't have to tell you his name, do I? My neighbor, I mean."

"If I need to know, I'll give you an opportunity to ask your friend for permission to give us his name," said Lew.

"You've been recovering for a long time?" said Osborne.

"Six years," said Blue with a nod of satisfaction. "Not always easy."

"No, it isn't," said Osborne. Blue gave him an inquiring glance and he nodded.

"Ah," she said. "So you've been there."

"Yep. I go to meetings here in Loon Lake."

"Is that how you know Ray Pradt?" asked Lew. "He indicated you two are friends."

"Y'know, I really can't answer that without being sure that Ray—"

"Tell you what," said Lew. "How 'bout I assume how you know Ray and we'll leave it at that. I'll assume you see him on occasion in Minocqua. I don't need to know where exactly."

"And that's true—when he's been guiding in the area I run into him. Great guy. Tells bad jokes but he's cute." Blue put out her cigarette and relaxed into her chair. Osborne was relieved when she didn't reach for another.

"Let's go back to my relationship with my mother. See, the conundrum of being my mother's daughter was that even as she didn't like me, even as she forced me to live away from home all those years —she saved my life. She kept me from being around people I was likely to drink with, which is why I'm here today. And I like being alive. So I have no compelling reason to want to hurt my mother."

"But she was forcing you into marriage."

"Oh, right. Look at me, Chief Ferris. Do I strike you as someone who could be forced into anything?"

"But—"

"I know what you've heard. Chances are the wedding was going to be called off. Barry and I kind of went along with the idea when our mothers cooked it up years ago while we were still in high school. Even then Barry and I both knew he was gay.

"But the thing is—his father doesn't. His father is very elderly, Barry loves him dearly and he is convinced that if his dad were to find out that he's gay—it could kill him. So we kept up the pretense when Barry was visiting and things kinda snowballed. Our mothers set that date. I'm okay with it—after all, isn't marriage supposed to be about friendship? We're good buddies."

Lew studied the girl's face, saying nothing. "Yes…well," said Blue, breaking the silence, "there is also the fact that I owe Barry and I will do whatever he needs me to. It was Barry who found me passed out at a party years ago and got me to an emergency room. If he hadn't, I would have died from alcohol poisoning. Like I said, I owe Barry."

"Blue, there has to be an easier way to pay that debt than marrying a man who would much prefer a different lifestyle," said Lew.

"It was only to last until his dad died—and he's ninety-six!"

"So your relationship with Barry, your pending marriage has nothing to do with money?"

Blue shook her head. "No. No matter what people might think. Barry and I are like brother and sister. I would do anything for him."

Lew flipped her notebook pages back as if looking for questions she had forgotten to ask. Osborne took the opening to ask the question that had been in the back of his mind since seeing the photo of the baby's face so carefully excised from the family album.

"Do you have any idea why Nolan hated—maybe that's too strong a word—why you say your mother didn't like you?"

"Hey, no, hate is a good word for it, Dr. Osborne,"

said Blue. "And, yes, I do know why. But, first, let me make some coffee. You guys want any?"

"Yes, please," said Lew and Osborne simultaneously. Osborne glanced out the window at a sky the color of duct tape—a little too dark for three in the afternoon. Oh, well, he thought, that's November for you. Thank the Lord for black coffee.

TWENTY-ONE

"WHEN I WAS A Little kid, there were times I'd turn quick and I'd catch my mother staring at me with this weird look on her face. It was a look that made me feel ugly from the inside out. In those days, too, I heard her tell people I was called 'Blue' because I was born premature and looking like a little old man—skinny and wrinkled. But that wasn't true. My grandfather called me 'Blue' from when I was a baby. He loved my eyes."

Blue pushed her chair back, crossed her legs and sipped from her coffee cup. Osborne had the sense she had told this story many times before. Lew sat listening, her eyes on Blue's face and no sense of urgency about her. Osborne knew from experience that she was happy to let Blue talk—and for as long as she needed. When they compared notes later, it could well be the words not said that might be most telling.

"It's not like she was angry all the time," said Blue, "but I never knew when she might turn on me. When she did it was a full-frontal assault—she would accuse me of lying, of stealing, of all sorts of bad behavior. When I tried to say I hadn't done anything, she would fly into a rage and come after me, start hitting me. If it hadn't been for Andy…

"It wasn't until I was older, in my early teens, that I would hear her insist that other people were telling lies about her, that they hated her, things I knew weren't true. By then I was old enough to understand paranoia and someone being emotionally ill, but not when I was a little kid. I was fifteen when I said to myself My mother is sick, her reality is not my reality and I am never going to be like her."

It must have been the serious expressions on their faces that prompted Blue to give a slight laugh and say, "Now, hold on. My entire life wasn't tragic. Grampa loved me. He was always happy to see me.

"Grampa was my mother's father. He knew she could be wacko so he made sure I spent a lot of time with him. Even when I was a toddler, I would live all summer at his house up here—the one Mom tore down. We'd go fishing and stuff. Sit in his porch swing together and watch the sun go down. It was wonderful—until Mom would arrive to take me home."

"What about your relationship with your father? Andy?" said Osborne, his voice cracking slightly as her words reminded him of his own distance from Mallory, his eldest who had been her mother's favorite and had seemed to shut him out. Only now were they finding their way towards each other: late, yes, but not too late, thank goodness.

"We weren't close when I was real little—he was in the background always but not real affectionate or anything. Andy's never been comfortable around young children. Thing I remember most from those days is that he would step in when Mom was hitting me and make her stop. And when I was in my teens and got in all the trouble, he stood by me."

Blue's face seemed to age as she spoke. The memories hardening her eyes, deepening the lines that years of tension had etched into her features. She had been young once but at the moment that was a long time ago. Osborne had seen a face like hers before: his own in the mirror during those months in rehab.

"Then one day Grampa wasn't well and Mother decided to take over the family business, which was a relief to me because all of a sudden she wasn't around to criticize all the time. I could breathe. She enrolled me in the same boarding school Barry was attending, Harmony Country Day.

"Now I had friends that Mom didn't know and couldn't say mean things about. That was the good part. The bad part was my friends were as confused as I was. My friends had parents who kept them in boarding school all winter, summer camp all summer and let them come home to empty houses on holiday weekends. Houses empty of people but well stocked with whiskey, beer and liqueurs. You better believe, they partied hard.

"That's when I started to drink. We made a concoction once that ate the porcelain off a kitchen sink. I drank to have fun, to not worry, to forget my awful mother. I mean, I wasn't the only kid with a screwed-up parent. Trust me. I considered myself lucky I didn't have some of the parents they did. Those were the days—Binge Drinking 101.

"I crashed during one of those weekend blowouts—

that was the night Barry got me to the hospital. Thank goodness he was there, too, because no one else was sober enough to get help. A couple days later, Mother and Andy met with the headmaster who said that I was a ringleader and Harmony Country Day would be better off without me.

"Oh, man, the next few weeks were awful. My mother spent hours telling me I was an embarrassment to the family, that I 'always did it'—meaning I always screwed up and she had no hope I would even make it into college."

Blue gave a little chuckle at that. "I did just graduate from UW Madison with honors so she was wrong on that point. But she packed me off to rehab in northern Minnesota and for four years I was not allowed back to our home in Lake Forest—except for one visit with my grandfather before he died. He made her let me come to see him. So we had a little time together. I was pretty shaky still."

Blue paused, her eyes misted as she said, "Bear with me now because I'll probably start to cry.

"Grampa was so tired and he knew he was dying. He gave me a framed portrait of my grandmother, who had died right after my mother was born so I never knew her. He showed me how I had her smile and her blue eyes. He said I was growing up to look just like her. She was very pretty. Do you know, that is the first time I began to feel like I could be pretty, too. Then he told me that he knew I was strong, that he knew I could make it through rehab and even though he didn't say it…" Blue paused, her voice cracking as she said, "I heard him forgive me."

"Did he tell you about your inheritance?" said Lew.

"No, he just said I needed to go to a good school because I was smart like him and could run a business someday. And he said not to let my mother get to me. He said that I was an heiress and she couldn't change that—but that's all he said about money. So I have no idea if I get five thousand or fifty thousand. From what I've overheard this summer, which is that my mother has lost a lot of money—I imagine that Andy and I will have to sell this place. And that's fine," said Blue with a wave of her hand, "I don't need all this.

"But I had a surprise for Grampa that day. I told him I knew the family secret."

"The family secret?" said Lew.

"Yes, I was a senior in high school, at a boarding school run by the rehab center, when I finally discovered why it was that my mother was always saying I had ruined her life."

"Blue," said Osborne, "before you say anything more, I need to know—why are you here? Why didn't you move away from your mother a long time ago?"

Blue gave some thought to his question, then waved a hand towards the window facing west. "The lake. I love this lake. It's in my bones. It fills my heart. And, remember, up until this summer I was away at college. I've managed to duck and cover. But let me finish— because this lucky thing happened just before Grampa died—and it changed my life."

"MY COUNSELOR AT THE rehab center was running late one day and I was waiting in her office when I saw my file on her desk. And I had this 'come to Jesus' moment—do I look? Do I not look?

"I looked. And what did I find? A copy of my birth certificate was in there and, surprise, Andrew Reece is not my father.

"So I asked Grampa about that. Who was the man whose name was on my birth certificate? Grampa said I was old enough to know the truth. That the summer my mother turned twenty she became pregnant by a local boy. He's dead now—died in a car accident years ago. Grampa and his second wife didn't believe in abortion or adoption—they wanted her married. But the guy who got her pregnant wouldn't have anything to do with that.

"Mother knew Andy from her chemistry class at Northwestern. I guess they had dated a couple times. Grampa offered him a lot of money to marry my mother and he agreed. Later, Grampa had to offer him even more money to stay married to her. He told me that Mother might not love Andy but she needed him. She was a nut case and he was stable. So that's the love story of Nolan and Andy Reece."

"Your grandfather told you all this?" said Lew.

"Yes. He said maybe he was wrong to have forced that marriage, forced my mother to have me—but having me around made it okay with him." Blue laughed.

"Now I had a better understanding of why Mother was so angry with me, but I didn't know what to do about it. Keep in mind I was eighteen and still living in the rehab community. Shortly after my grandfather died, my regular therapist became ill and I was assigned to a different psychologist, a woman who specialized in working with people with personality disorders.

"She was very interested in hearing about my mother—her mood swings, her accusations, the paranoia, the rages. She was the first person who wanted to hear every detail. She asked lots of questions, I cried. But when we were done, she gave me a big hug and sat me down to explain that none of my mother's behavior was my fault. She couldn't tell me the source of my mother's problems. Was she schizophrenic? Was she bi-polar? Had she been normal as child but changed in adolescence? No answers to that.

"But the psychologist had this great line—she said 'Blue, you have to understand that people with personality disorders think that they're perfectly normal—and you're nuts. You are never going to convince them otherwise.' Those are the words that changed my life.

"All of a sudden I could step back and see my mother with new eyes. I could take that abusive behavior and set it aside. I could try to find a few things about her that I could like—maybe even love."

"And?" said Lew.

"I'm working on it," said Blue with a rueful smile. "Maybe her good taste?"

"Her interest in helping the Dark Sky sisters," said Osborne.

"I have a hard time with that," said Blue. "Frances I can deal with even though you can barely carry on a conversation with her—but that Josie. Mother adored her. I dunno, I guess if I'm fair, I'd have to say they were Mother's way of feeling needed.

"Now, please, I've been through enough therapy to be honest with myself so I'm working hard to get past my feelings about Josie. It's not her fault that Mother made such a deal over her. Mother's death, Mildred murdered—those poor girls are so alone right now and I feel sorry for them. So I'm trying. I was happy to help out last night. They needed a place to stay and there was plenty of room over at the Murphys'. The last thing either one of them needs right now is for me to come down on them. Still," said Blue with a wry grin, "it was Frances who helped me with breakfast.

"And it's Mother who kept shoving Josie at me. Not Josie herself. That's why I showed you her room and the album and made you sit through my emotional history here—because I think it's critical that you see what an emotionally disturbed person my mother was. But while she couldn't hurt me—not anymore—that doesn't mean she didn't hurt others. She did. Sometimes I could stop her, sometimes Andy could. But we weren't around her all the time."

"She was hard on the people working here? The housekeeper, the caretaker?"

"Yes, she could be nice one minute—holler at them the next. But I don't think anyone here would have hurt her. They figured out how to manage her...plus she paid them well."

"She paid them to be abused," said Lew.

"You could put it that way."

"Andy, too?"

"Oh, yes, but he was artful at avoiding her." Blue

lowered her voice and pointed towards the door to the den, reminding them that Andy was just a room away.

"He doesn't know, by the way, that you know he's not your father," whispered Lew.

"He does now. Just before you and Dr. Osborne got here today, he tried to tell me. He was afraid that it would come out in the investigation and upset me. I told him I've known for years. He was pretty shocked."

"That's why you're calling him 'Andy' instead of 'Dad'?" said Osborne.

"You noticed," said Blue, surprised.

"That's why Doc's here," said Lew, throwing Osborne an appreciative glance. "I listen for the answers to my questions while he's an ear for things I may miss. But, tell me, Blue, why didn't you tell Andy that you knew about your adoption a long time ago?"

"I was afraid he might tell Mother that I knew and who knows what fresh hell that might have caused. I saw no reason to rock the boat."

A sudden commotion outside—a loud thumping accompanied by the barking of dogs, caused all three to leap from their chairs and run to the kitchen door. The green pick-up had pulled in next to Lew's cruiser and was idling. Two golden retrievers raced back and forth in the truck's deep-walled bed while three heads could be seen inside the extended cab. The two in the front seat were bouncing to strains of raucous music. The third head was bent, pushing its way past the front seat to the door.

TWENTY-TWO

ONE OF THE silhouetted heads turned out to be Frances Dark Sky, who was struggling to get out of the truck's rear seat. She jumped from the passenger side only to turn an ankle as she landed, ending up on hands and knees. Before Osborne could rush down the porch steps to give her a hand, she had leapt to her feet.

"Frances, are you okay?" said Blue from behind Osborne. Frances gave an embarrassed wave of her hand and stepped back from the truck, eyes on the ground.

The driver's side door opened slowly, music blaring into the deepening shadows of the afternoon. Out popped a short, chunky man with a head that seemed massive thanks to a halo of blonde curls in desperate need of a trim. He wore a denim jacket, the kind lined with fake sheepskin, which hung open to expose a shapeless gray wool sweater and baggy jeans riding low on his hips. Osborne guessed him to be somewhere in his early to mid-twenties.

"Jake Cahak?" said Lew, stepping down from the porch steps and advancing towards the man. "I'm Chief Ferris with the Loon Lake Police—like to ask you a few questions."

"Yep, I'm Jake," said the man with a grin. Opening

his mouth exposed a cluster of bottom teeth rearranged by forces other than nature. An upper right incisor was missing as well. None of that affected his ability to chew as he managed to chomp away on a wad of gum. As Lew approached the truck, he thrust both hands into his jacket pockets and waited, eyes skittish as he looked from Lew to Osborne and back to Lew. "Just giving the girls here a ride over from the Murphy place."

Lew walked to the back of the truck. "Big dogs. Friendly?"

"Yep. Them's the Reeces'. They love everbody. Just picked 'em up at the kennel. Okay, to bring 'em back here, ain't it?" He looked past Osborne to where Blue was standing. "Thought your old man said it was okay. Right?"

"That's fine," said Blue. "You can let them out, Jake."

"And this here's Josie and Frances," said Jake as Josie let herself down from the high front seat of the truck. She dusted at the jeans she was wearing then turned a bright face towards Lew.

"I know Josie and Frances," said Lew, her voice quiet and level. "This your truck or does it belong to the Reeces?"

"Oh, no, this is my baby," said Jake, laying an affectionate hand on the door handle to the driver's side.

"Good for you," said Lew. "Trucks like this don't come cheap. You live around here, Jake?"

"Got a place over in the cities," said Jake, pointing to the west as if Minneapolis would suddenly pop up behind a stand of balsam, "but stay right down the road most of the time." He tipped his head towards the drive. "Job comes with a cabin about a third of a mile that way."

"And is that where you were the night before last?" Lew asked. "During the engagement party?"

"Oh, hell, no. I dropped the girls off and went on down to Jimmy's Bar. Had a pizza, watched the...ah, the Bears game. Hung out there 'til Josie called and said it was time to take 'em home."

"So you were at Jimmy's, the bar right down the road here?"

"Yep."

"When can Francie and I go home, Chief Ferris?" said Josie, her whine interrupting Lew. "Do we have to stay here tonight? And my cell phone—when I can get my phone back?"

"Young lady," said Lew, "I made it clear to you yesterday that you'll be allowed back in Mildred Taggert's house when the crime lab has finished inspecting the property and—"

Before she could say more, the dogs set up another round of loud barking as a man emerged from the woods behind the garage. "Now who the hell?" Jake spun around. As he did, he reached into a long toolbox resting in the bed of his truck and pulled out a shotgun.

"Hey, take it easy. Put that gun down," said Lew as Ray approached, the stuffed trout askew on his head, its earflaps down leaving the ties to flutter in the wind. No parka for Ray—he looked bulky but warm in layers of T-shirts over which he had pulled a worn red sweatshirt emblazoned with the slogan: Vegetarian: Old Indian word for Poor Hunter.

"You're looking at one of my deputies, Ray Pradt.

Mr. Cahak, did you hear me? Gun goes back in the truck—and what are you doing with an uncased gun in there anyway? That's against the law, fella."

"Whaddya mean? I'm security here. And damned spooked after what's happened if you don't mind my saying so."

"No, Jake," said Blue from the porch stairs, "you're not security. You're the caretaker."

"Same goddamn thing."

"Put the gun in its case and put it back in your truck," said Lew. "This time—it's a warning. Next time, it's a fine and ten days in the Loon Lake jail."

"Good food in the hoosegow," offered Ray with a grin.

Turning towards the truck, Jake mumbled under his breath but everyone heard him anyway as he said, "Oh, yeah, I forgot. Loon Lake's got women for cops."

With that Osborne wondered if the guy wouldn't be better off shooting himself instead of putting the gun away. Lew ignored the comment, waiting in silence as Jake rustled around until he located a canvas gun bag, slipped the gun inside, zipped it shut and laid it back in the toolbox.

Then he turned to Ray who was now standing near-by. "How far did you go back in there? That's trespassing on private land, bud, and I worked damn hard planting young balsam all along that property line, so I don't need no dumb shit tramping down all them saplings."

Lew opened her mouth to speak but Ray raised a finger to stop her.

"Well...gotta tell ya," said Ray, sounding as if he was just this side of a laugh, "I do know a new tree from an old tree so don't you worry. Nothing disturbed. Now—" he raised a cautionary hand as Jake looked like he was about to unload again "—you asked what I was doing back there so let me tell you.

"Just as I was looking through those fancy cars they got parked in front of the garage there at the request of Chief Ferris—given this is a crime scene some of that has to happen, y'know—well...I happened to look up and guess what I saw staring at me? Standing right by the drive there...a seven...point...buck. No kidding, man, that is premium venison.

"So, sir—" Ray waved a hand as if to forgive Jake his stupid behavior "—I understand your concern—no matter that. But tell you what—" he leaned toward the shorter man conspiratorially "—I followed that critter and stumbled onto some darn decent deer trails running back that way—" Ray turned and took his time to point towards the woods from where he had just emerged "—so took a few minutes to check 'em out. Season's open, y'know." Ray raised his eyebrows as he grinned with anticipation.

"Not for you—this is private land. No one hunts there." As he spoke, Jake took a step toward Ray, then stopped with his feet apart, hands on his hips.

"You are so belligerent," said Ray with a laugh. "I'm just trying to point you in the right direction."

"Now hold on, you two," said Blue, running down the porch stairs. "Jake, Ray is a friend of mine. He can hunt this property if he wants."

Jake threw up his hands in defeat, "All right, all right, whatever you say. Jes' tryin' to do my job."

"Hey, you razzbonya," said Ray as Blue walked over to him. He put one arm around her shoulders and ran his knuckles lightly over her head as he said, "Nothin' like a Chinese haircut—you feelin' better?"

"Yeah," said Blue with a slow smile and a shy eye that brought youth back into her face.

Jake moved to stand near Josie where he started bouncing lightly on his toes as if to keep his feet warm. Osborne watched as Jake bounced back behind Josie and with a quick motion slipped both his hands into the back pockets of her jeans.

"Hey!" she squealed, "stop that now." She slapped half-heartedly at the invading hands and Jake backed off, blowing on his bare fingers.

"Jes' tryin' to keep warm," he said with an impish grin. Osborne glanced over at Frances who was standing at distance from her sister and Jake, her arms crossed to pull her parka tight against the cold. She had seen Jake's move. Her eyes were wary and worried. She was not amused.

The porch door banged open and Andy Reece stepped out of the house. "Jake, you're back. Great—I need you inside right away. This new computer I got—can't figure how to hook it into the router. Got a big bet going on a bass tournament in Arkansas and if I can't get online, I may lose a couple thousand. Come on in and get me fixed up, will ya?"

That was all Jake needed to hear. Before Lew could stop him, he had run up the steps past Andy. Blue

motioned for the girls to follow. "Frances, Josie—
come inside while Jake gets Dad fixed up. You're
freezing out here."

Lew waited for the door to close behind Frances,
who lingered as if reluctant to follow her sister inside.
Her eyes caught Osborne's for a brief second and he
wondered if she had something she wanted to say. But
she looked away just as quickly and followed the others into the house.

"Andy, how long has Cahak worked for you?"
asked Lew.

"Oh, 'bout a year now," said Andy, standing with
the door open, eager to get back into the house. "Nolan
hired an electrical contractor from the cities to design
the computer systems that run the sound and lighting
in the house. Jake was one of his guys. We kept him on
because he knows what to do when things go haywire.
Guy grew up on Lake Minnetonka—so he's good at
servicing all the boats, too.

"He actually asked us for the job," said Andy.
"Told us he loves to hunt and fish and could take care
of the basics around here. Been a godsend for me
every time that damn Internet goes down. Blue thinks
I'm a gadget geek but that guy knows computers like
you wouldn't believe."

AS THE PORCH DOOR closed behind Andy, Ray waved
Lew and Osborne away from the house and over
towards the garage. "Follow me back here, will you?"

"Sounds like you found something?" asked Lew in
a low tone.

"Plenty," said Ray. They rounded the back of the garage to where Ray had set down two paper evidence bags and a two-by-four nearly three feet long.

"I started in from where we saw those tracks on the shoreline and did we get lucky. The deer have been feeding and you know how they leave jagged edges on everything. Well, whoever's been back in there was wearing a burgundy and tan sweater because I found strands of yarn on a scattering of brush from the lake-side all the way up to the driveway. Whoever it was had to have ripped the hell out of their sweater, which means…to me anyway…they were running. Could have been running in the dark, which is why they bar-reled through brush like that. I harvested what I could find, marked the brush so you can see the pattern and put the strands of yarn in here." He handed one of the evidence bags to Lew.

"But the pièce de résistance…" Ray paused to pick up the second bag and open it for Lew and Osborne to peer inside.

"Rubber gloves?" said Osborne, staring at the black gloves inside the bag.

"Yep, found 'em shoved under a dead tree not far from the lake along with this big stick. Interesting, huh."

"Let's get back to the cruiser so I can check in with Doug Jesperson," said Lew. "I hope he hasn't left town yet. Like to see what he thinks the lab can do with those gloves and that two-by-four. Good work, Ray. Very good work."

"You're as welcome as the flowers, Chief. Mind if I

head out now? I promised to take Gina to fish fry tonight and I…need to clean up. You two feel like joining us?"

"We'll be there," said Lew. "I already told Doc his dinner's on me. You get going, I'll call Doug Jesperson right now."

TWENTY-THREE

"RUBBER GLOVES?" said Doug when Lew reached him on the police radio in the cruiser. "That could be a bonus, Lewellyn—if they were used by the killer. People think if they use rubber gloves that they won't leave prints and they won't. Better than that—they leave skin cells, DNA! But in order to have any match, we need to collect samples from any suspects you may have."

"That's why I'm calling. How soon can you get out here? I've got five people on-site right now, any one of whom might—"

"Now?" Doug sounded exasperated. "This couldn't wait until Monday? Half my holiday is shot already."

"I thought you told me you volunteered for holidays, Doug. Come on now, no one handles evidence better than you and your team. Maybe send one of your people out here. I'll keep everyone waiting."

Silence. "All right, I'll ask Bruce if he minds heading back your way."

"Thank you very much," said Lew. "I'll wait for him. But, Doug, how long will it take to do the DNA testing?"

"We use private contractors these days. If I'm lucky I can find someone who'll rush it through. Maybe a week or two?"

"No sooner than that?"

"You've been watching too much TV. Now, Lewellyn, we're just about finished here," said Doug, "but a couple things you need to know. First, we didn't even try to dust for prints in the shop. So many people walk in and out of there, pick up stuff, lean on the counter—no point to it. We did dust the cash register. Have not removed the computer the old lady used for licenses—it's specific to that purpose so I see no reason to rip it out of the countertop. And, yes, we dusted it for prints. Thing is, you didn't tell me about the barn."

"What about it?"

"You didn't go to the second floor?"

"Doug, our investigation kept us there until close to midnight last night. Right or wrong, I chose to interrogate the neighbors. No, I did not go to the second floor of the barn. But I will—why?"

"It's fully remodeled. Place looks like shit outside but the inside has been completely renovated. All new windows, the walls rebuilt. Two big fully furnished bedrooms and a study. One of the neighbors said your other victim, Nolan Reece, paid for the renovation. Wanted those girls to have a nice home. We've combed through there but nothing of note to report until we have lab results."

"Are you saying I can let them back inside tonight?"

"I think so. I'll know pretty soon if we've covered everything here. The first floor of the barn has been used strictly as a garage—the old lady parked that ancient Chevy of hers in there. But there is one odd thing that you need to watch out for. That upstairs study is wired for hi-speed Internet access with a router in place—but no computer. See if you can find the computer. Has to be one somewhere, otherwise—why the expense, y'know?"

"You got the girls' cell phones that I left with the sheriff's deputy?"

"We did. We're heading into the weekend so not sure how quickly we can get back to you on that. You know, Lewellyn, if you listened to my jokes…"

"Maybe next time, Doug," said Lew, grimacing at Osborne. Jesperson grunted. "Seriously, I do appreciate you're being willing to take the time there today."

"Oh, and one more thing—the lab called me an hour ago. They identified the shavings under the nails of the Reece woman. Marine paint, sapphire blue."

OSBORNE LET MIKE out of the yard and walked behind the dog down to the shoreline. He folded his arms to rest elbows and forearms on a section of dock, which had been pulled onshore and upended against a tree in preparation for the blasts of winter: furious winds determined to shovel slabs of ice up onto the banks of the lake.

As the dog ran sniffing after hints of squirrels and rabbits, Osborne leaned forward, chin on his gloved hands, ready to savor the early sunset. He could never get over the fact that late November days ended before five o'clock. So dark, so soon.

Enough light remained for him to see that even though there was open water a hundred feet out, ice now glazed the surfaces close to shore. But at the moment he was less interested in the spreading ice than thinking back over the last half hour he and Lew had spent at the Reeces'.

Lew, as eager as Osborne to end the long day, had made short order of the DNA sampling. True to his word, Jesperson had dispatched one of the young crime lab assistants who had arrived within fifteen minutes of the conversation between Chief Ferris and his boss. Once Lew made the point that everyone attending the party would have to be swabbed for DNA samples, no one had resisted except Jake Cahak.

He made the lame argument that he wasn't invited to the dinner but Lew reminded him he had been on the premises that night. With a shrug, he had agreed. After the samples were taken, Lew checked with Jesperson one more time and was relieved to hear that the Dark Sky sisters could return to Mildred's. That was when she said that since she had to drop Osborne off to get his car—she might as well give the girls a ride to town, too.

Leaning on the dock, Osborne thought back over that moment. Had he seen disappointment on Jake's face? Or was he reading too much into the man's expressions? He made a mental note to ask Lew if she had noticed a change when he learned he wouldn't be the girls' driver this time.

She may not have, as her attention had been drawn to Josie, who was lugging more than the overnight case and purse that Frances was carrying.

"Josie, what is that?" Lew had said as the girls were climbing into the back seat of the cruiser. She pointed to a flat plastic case that Josie had slung over one shoulder—bright blue with yellow and orange flowers.

"Oh, this? Just my school laptop," said Josie.

"You have a computer in there?"

"Uh-huh." Josie set the case on her lap and looked out the window as if the discussion was ended. Lew left it at that for the moment and turned the ignition key.

The four of them drove in silence until Lew turned onto Highway C. Then Josie had leaned forward from the back seat to say, "Chief Ferris, I remembered something that happened before dinner the other night."

"Yes…" Lew waited to hear.

Osborne turned sideways, eyes on Josie as she spoke. "I…well…I don't want to get anyone in trouble."

Lew glanced up at the rearview mirror to catch Josie's expression and said, "Withholding information that might be important to the investigation is not wise, Josie. You can end up in more trouble than you might expect. Does this involve Jake Cahak?"

"No," the girl said. Osborne saw Frances give her sister a look of surprise. "Blue and her mom had a big argument. Up in the guesthouse. I heard because I was in the bathroom fixing my hair."

"Did you hear this, too, Frances?" said Lew.

"No," said Frances in a low voice. "I wasn't there."

"Josie, what was the argument about—could you tell?"

"Yes, it was about money," said Josie. "I couldn't hear it all but Blue was real mad because her mother wouldn't give her some. The door was closed so I couldn't hear all the words real clear—but Blue screamed at her, then stomped out."

"This was before the party?"

"It was when the party was just getting started 'cause Blue got there late. Her mom was real mad about that."

"Maybe that's what the argument was all about," said Lew.

"No. I heard them screaming at each other about money," said Josie. "Mrs. Reece was shouting that she knew Blue was stealing money from her—maybe her purse or something? I couldn't hear more than that."

"They fought a lot, didn't they?" said Lew.

"Not really," said Frances, shifting on the car seat as if to distance herself from her sister. "Mrs. Reece could get pretty mean sometimes—to Blue and to Mr. Reece. But they were good about it." Frances looked at Josie. "I never heard Blue get mad at her mother."

"You weren't there in the bathroom that night," said Josie. "I know what I heard."

"Whatever." Frances turned her face away from her sister to stare out the car window.

Lew had decided to drop the girls off first and pulled into the drive alongside the door to the shop. "Mr. Jesperson from the Wausau Crime Lab said that he made sure the keys were left on the store counter. I'll wait here to be sure you can get inside okay and in the morning, I'll stop by. I would like to see all the work that's been done in the barn for you girls. Is that where you sleep?"

"Josie sleeps there," said Frances. "I like my room in the house."

As Josie opened the car door to get out, Lew reached back over the seat and said, "I'll take your laptop, Josie. You can leave that on the seat there."

Josie clutched the case to her chest. "No, I have all my school work on this. I have to have it." She was getting out of the car when Lew nudged Osborne. He opened the car door and stepped out to block Josie's way.

"We'll be very careful with it, Josie," he said as he reached for the case, wondering if he would have to fight her for it. But she let the strap slip off her shoulder without resisting, a pout on her face.

Back in the cruiser after the girls entered the house, Lew looked over at Osborne and said, "Looks like we found the missing computer, doesn't it? Jesperson's not going to let me forget that I should've checked for this. Damn, I hate it when I overlook the obvious, you know?"

"Thing is, Lew," said Osborne trying hard to remember the scene at Mildred's as Blue picked up the girls. "I don't think Josie had it with her that night. You had each girl pack an overnight bag and they each had a purse. I'm almost sure of that."

"You're right, Doc. I don't remember seeing the case she carries it in either. She certainly didn't leave it at the Reeces' either because we would have seen it."

"Guess you need to run this down to Wausau in the morning?" said Osborne.

"Let me talk to Gina first," said Lew. "She does computer forensics. Rather pay for her time than that creep Jesperson."

"I don't blame you."

OSBORNE PUSHED BACK from the dock. He had an hour to shower and change before fish fry. Before calling the dog, he studied the ice along the shore where the setting sun had turned it rose pink. The fading light highlighted a series of circles that each held their own center with ripples radiating out. Were those caused by miniature springs bubbling up from the lake bottom? Or had a late hatch of insects enticed fish circling just under the thin crust of ice?

The thought of the insects reminded him of his winter surprise for Lew: he was going to use his own new laptop computer, a birthday gift from his daughters, to visit the Wisconsin Fly Fisherman's Web site every week. Once there, he would go to their database of "Aquatic Insects of Wisconsin Trout Streams" with a goal of memorizing two names for each of the stoneflies listed: the Latin family name and the insect's common name. Next winter he would do the mayflies and the winter after that—the caddisflies.

Or maybe just their common names. He had yet to determine how hard his plan was going to be. The Latin terms might be a struggle as it had been too many years since he had studied Latin in high school. But the insects' common names were enchanting—so provocative they should be easy to remember: Pale Evening Dun, Black Quill, Summer Golden, Yellow Eyes, White Wulff, Blank Dance...

Yep, if he did this right, he might not cast like an expert but he sure could sound like one.

Smiling at the thought, he called the dog. "Here, Mike. Time for us to shower. Friday night, doncha know—fish fry!"

TWENTY-FOUR

THE LOON LAKE PUB was bustling, with every table in sight filled. Brass sconces along the walls cast a warm glow making it easy to forget the freezing temperatures outdoors. A happy buzz of voices peppered with occasional hoots of laughter put a smile on Osborne's face as he and Lew entered the bar fronting the dining room. A shout from one of the tables near the back caught their attention—Ray and Gina had already arrived and commandeered a table for four.

Given it was Friday night, Ray—on behalf of everyone at the table—had waived a need for menus and no one argued: fish fry for all. As Osborne leaned towards the waitress to order frosted mugs of Leinenkugel's Red for the ladies and Cokes for himself and Ray, he saw two hands park themselves on Lew's shoulders. Ralph Steadman, his chest expansive in a green and gold plaid Pendleton wool shirt, his white beard neatly trimmed to emphasize his perpetual sportsman's tan, loomed over their table.

Great, thought Osborne, just when the evening was off to a wonderful start, this razzbonya has to show up. He did not return Ralph's big fat grin.

"Chief Lewellyn Ferris," said Ralph, bending so

close he threatened to nuzzle Lew's ear. He spoke with more than a hint of an English accent, which always struck Osborne as pretentious. It was Osborne's personal opinion, shared with his McDonald's buddies on more than one occasion, that since the man's parents had moved to the U.S. when Ralph was four, he'd had plenty of time to lose the accent. Plenty of time.

"Have you made up your mind about our fly fishing trip to Jackson Hole?" said Ralph. "Tough to turn that freebie down—it's going to be a hell of a trip…"

"I have indeed," said Lew, pushing her chair back to gaze up at him with smiling eyes. "Not only am I planning to go but—" she extended her left hand toward Osborne "—I've invited Doc here to join me. He can pick up a lot more fly fishing expertise on that trip than I can ever teach him."

A shadow crossed Ralph's face. "But there's only two openings."

"Last time I checked there were only two of us," said Lew, indicating herself and Osborne.

"Oh," said Ralph, taken aback. Osborne knew right then that the jerk had planned for himself to be Number Two. Sorry, guy.

"Doc knows, of course, the entire trip is on horseback?"

"He sure does," said Lew as Osborne nodded in agreement.

"Well, in that case you two better start training. Doc, when was the last time you were on a horse?"

Osborne pursed his lips, thinking. "Oh, fifty years ago, maybe."

"The ride in is twenty-two miles. That's a bit of a ride even for a cowboy." Ralph was not going to give up easy.

"How long a ride is that?" said Lew. "Must be several hours at least."

"Six and a half. If the weather holds."

"Six and a half hours straight on horseback?" Lew's eyes widened. "You didn't tell me that part."

"I told you to expect serious backcountry fishing," said Ralph. "Here's some advice, you two. The outfitter recommends that first-timers wear panty hose—helps minimize the saddle sores. Doc, I think you'll want to go for a woman's extra extra large."

"You're putting us on, right?" said Osborne. Ray and Gina had covered their mouths with their napkins.

"Oh, come on, Ralph," said Lew. "Did you wear panty hose when you went?"

"I haven't made this trip, Chief. That's why it was offered to the store. They're trying to build business because it's such a rugged go. But worth it—you'll fish the Buffalo, Atlantic Creek—maybe the Thoroughfare. Famous trout water. And everything is packed in by the outfitter—tents, food, latrine, bear spray, you name it—all you need to bring is your fishing gear."

"And panty hose," said Lew with a lift of her eyebrows. "Wish you'd told me that part."

"Enjoy your dinner, folks," said Ralph, looking as satisfied as a walleye that had swallowed two minnows without getting hooked, "gotta get back to my table or my wife'll kill me."

Lew waited until Ralph was out of hearing range before she said, "He made that up—the panty hose part. I know I'm sure as hell not riding six hours in the heat of July in panty hose."

"Six and a half hours," said Ray. "No, I don't think he is wrong on that. I've guided a few fellas who've been on hunting trips where you go by horse into the backcountry for elk. I can tell ya they were a l-o-o-n-g time recovering, doncha know. If you like, I'll check with one of 'em—see what he suggests."

"Please," said Osborne. "Woman's extra extra large. God help me!"

NEAR THE END of a meal that was as delicious as ever—the consensus of the group was that only Ray could sauté walleye or bluegill better than the chef at the Pub—Lew broke the promise she had made to Osborne when he'd picked her up earlier.

"I know I promised no work talk tonight," she said as she lifted her fork to cut into a slice of lemon meringue pie, "but I have a favor to ask of Gina."

"Go right ahead," said Gina, diving into her own wedge of pie. "I've had an excellent day capped off with an evening with good friends. I am in the mood to bestow multiple favors. What do you need?"

"The Wausau boys had already headed south when I found that one of the Dark Sky sisters had her laptop with her still. I had hoped that all the cell phones and computers connected with both investigations would be in their hands for analysis. Any chance I could send Josie's home with you and have you take a look at what she might have—or not have—on the hard drive?"

"Better yet," said Gina, "you're talking high school kid, right?"

"Sophomore."

"Let's see where she's been going online, too. That's where you'll get the best read on the kid. iTunes, eBay, Facebook—I'd love to see what she's up to. In fact, it fits in a funny way with my work on the stolen credit cards because just today we reached an agreement with the local ISPs and their lawyers to the point that I've narrowed our search to a final twenty-two locations selling fishing licenses. I noticed that Mildred's Food Shop is on the list. I doubt Josie's laptop has anything to do with our search but at least I'll know we've examined all the computers in use at that location."

"I'm not sure what else you need," said Lew, "but the crime lab has finished their work at Mildred's place so we can check the shop out easily in the morning. Does that make sense?"

"Yes, I'm interested in her place and the neighbors. We're beginning to think that we may have innocent merchants with lousy firewalls and outdated security software that have outsiders siphoning off their electronic data. I've gotta believe a little shop like your victim's is a classic example. At the very least, her place will give me a baseline for our investigation up here."

"What about you, Doc?" said Ray, turning to Osborne. "I'm gonna fight that ice in the morning for one last day of muskie fishing. Wanna come along?"

"Nope," said Osborne, "Chief needs me. We're expecting Blue Reece's fiancé and his parents to fly in

first thing. Last on our list of people who were at the
dinner party the other night—right, Lew?"

"Doc, I had a call from the switchboard just
before you arrived. The winter storm that's due to hit
us late tomorrow has shut down Chicago's O'Hare
airport. The Murphys have changed their flights to
arrive Sunday morning." She gave him a wicked
grin. "I see no reason you shouldn't take the morning to fish with Ray."

"Hey, old man—" Ray hit Osborne in the arm "—you
gotta come. No more muskie until next spring, y'know.
My boat's ready, I got plenty of hot coffee. And I figure we'll fish those—"

"Jeez, Ray," said Osborne, "you and I both know
this is the worst time of the year for muskie action and
it's going to be damn cold tomorrow."

"You're right, Doc. No time for sissies."

"You mean guys who wear panty hose?"

"N-o-o-o. That's not what I mean. We may be one of
two boats out there but at least it'll be all us true sportsmen. 'Cuz, Doc, you gotta remember that if we do see
a muskie—it'll be a lunker. A super lunker. This time of
year, those females are heavy with eggs and winter fat.
We got huge fish out there—and you know it, Doc."

"Is he right?" said Gina. "Or does misery love company?"

"No, he's right," said Osborne. "My argument is
that you may have monsters out there but they're
canny and their metabolism is slow and—"

"So I stocked up on live suckers and chubs and
packed up my plugs—Suick, Eddie, Pikie Minnow,

Cisco Kid, Rapala, Swim Whizz, Bobbie baits and a nice new Rizzo Diver. And a Slammer—"

"Enough," said Osborne, "you've twisted my arm. I'll go, I'll go."

Ray gave him a happy grin, eyes snapping with anticipation. "I won't make too big a thing of it, Doc. I figure we'll fish from late morning to one or so. Not too long. And just one spot—out by the big boulder. I spotted some green weeds out there."

"If you bring the coffee, I'll bring egg salad sandwiches," said Osborne, feeling a little more enthused. Fishing with Ray wasn't just fishing—you got a lot of freebies, too. Like good stories and new bad jokes. Plus, he wouldn't mind catching the biggest muskie of his life. A man is never too old to thrill to the landing of a really, really big fish.

As they walked to their cars after dinner, Osborne glanced across Main Street towards the sports bar where the young crowd liked to hang out. Pick-up after pick-up lined Loon Lake's main drag on that side of the street.

"Is that Jake Cahak's Dodge over there?" said Osborne as he opened the car door for Lew. She stood up to check. "Yes, that's his license plate. You can't miss that."

Osborne had to agree: BIG DOG does stand out.

"Something else, Doc," she said as she slipped into the passenger seat. "It was bugging me that I didn't get Josie's laptop sooner so I gave her a call late this afternoon and asked her how she happened to have it today since Mildred's place was secured before they left with Blue last night. She said Jake had had it since last weekend. She needed a new DVD drive and Nolan arranged for him to install one for her. So you were right—she didn't leave the house with it that night. And if I had checked the barn, I wouldn't have found it either."

"Make you feel better?"

"Nah, Jesperson will find some way to make an issue of it, I'm sure."

"An excuse to tell you another dirty joke." Lew punched him in the arm.

TWENTY-FIVE

THE DAY WAS CLASSIC November: the sky a flat steel gray and winds blowing fifteen to twenty out of the north. Heads down, Osborne and Ray heaved the bassboat over the ice until it fell through about eight feet from shore. The lake was so low Ray had to row another twenty feet and touch bottom with an oar until he was confident the water was deep enough to drop his 100-horse Mercury. As Ray throttled forward, Osborne wondered if two pair of long underwear might not have been wise.

Waves spraying off the sides of the boat, they neared the marker set out to prevent the loss of propellers to the monster rocks lurking below. Ray knew just where he wanted to anchor and did so. Within minutes they were casting, the wind to their back. Osborne scanned the lake in all directions. They were the only boat on the lake. True sportsmen or complete idiots?

No action. After twenty minutes, Ray changed his lure but Osborne had an old Rapala crank-bait that felt good when he cast so he stuck with it. His hopes of landing a fish had been high as they set out that morning but were sinking by the minute. Another half hour of no strikes confirmed his hunch that the shark of the north was nestled snug in the weeds below and not in the mood for teasing.

Even Ray's enthusiasm waned as the promised one o'clock hour neared. That plus Osborne's confession that his feet were freezing despite heavy socks and Sorel boots helped them make up their minds: time to eat lunch then call it a day.

Two sandwiches and the dregs of the coffee thermos later, Ray moved to start up the Mercury. He throttled forward...no movement. Again he throttled. The boat did not move.

"Do you think the wind pushed us a little too far over?" said Osborne. Ray tried again. No use. The chilled fishermen stared at each other and neither had to say a word. Under normal conditions, the area near the marker was hazardous. But with the lake as low as it was this year, it was even worse: the sunken boulders were poised to take hostages.

Ray put the outboard in Reverse, then Forward. Nope. He could not budge the hull off the rock. After thirty minutes of intermittent attempts, he sat down and pulled out his cell phone. "Doc, who do we call? We gotta find somebody to pull us off here."

"Do you even have cell service?"

Ray checked. "Yes, thank goodness. But I sure as hell can't call you, can I? Gina doesn't know how to run a boat. Most of my buddies are out deer hunting."

"Mine, too," said Osborne, a sudden image of the hunting shack's hot pot belly stove making him rue his decision not to hunt. "I would try Erin," said Osborne, "but she and Mark are in Milwaukee with the kids, visiting his grandparents."

"Lew?"

"I hate to do that, she's so busy as it is."

"Not to mention we'll look like fools."

"Speak for yourself," said Osborne. He wasn't the jabone who had insisted on fishing in these conditions.

"Hey, I got the ticket," said Ray, pointing an index finger to the sky. "I'll call the Birchwood Bar—see if there's anybody watching the football game that'd be willing to get us—for a six-pack."

"Good idea," said Osborne. "Be grateful the Packers aren't playing."

In less than fifteen minutes, a weathered pontoon with a 150-horse motor was barreling through the waves towards them. A stocky guy in an Army parka with a black knit cap pulled down over his ears waved at Ray, then tossed a yellow strap with a hook at one end their way. "Yo, Ray," he called over the wind, "you are gonna owe me for this, big guy."

"Who is that?" said Osborne as Ray wedged the hook in tight and raised the propeller so it would clear the rock as the boat moved.

"You don't know Clarence? He lives north of the Wisconsin River up on Highway G. Drives a school bus in the winter, works construction in the summer. Good man."

The good man was more than deserving of his six-pack. Under a black, scruffy beard Clarence was still red-faced from the wind when they took their seats at the bar. Ray was true to his word on the six-pack, threw in a promise of a day's ice fishing and Clarence was more than pleased.

"So you drive a school bus, Clarence?" said Osborne, warming his feet outside his boots. He was so chilled he'd ordered herbal tea, which he never drank—but it sounded hot and harmless.

"Yep," said Clarence. "Been drivin' for twenty-six years. Get to retire in four."

He took a swig from his beer then set the bottle down on the bar. "Yep, been a good job. I like the kids."

"You drive for St. Mary's or the public schools?"

"The high school. The teenagers. I got that serious look—" Clarence scowled at Osborne and Ray "—so I can scare the bejesus out of any that get under my nerves, y'know? But I tell you—" he banged his bottle so hard on the bar, the beer fizzed over the top "—things have changed in twenty-five years. Too many kids go home to empty houses these days, and you know where that takes you. Man, oh, man."

"I can imagine," said Osborne, shaking his head in agreement. "More drugs, more fooling around."

"Yep. When you drive a bus, you hear it all. They forget you're there, y'know."

"Really," said Ray. "What's the strangest thing you've heard recently?" He caught Osborne's eye over Clarence's head: this was turning into a fun afternoon.

"You two hear about that rich woman that was killed over on Lily Pond Road?"

"Heard a little," said Ray. "What'd you hear?"

"Well, those two Indian girls that live with old Mildred—they ride my bus. The young one, Josie, she's been bragging to her friends that she'll inherit a million bucks from that Reece woman someday. Looks like her day's come sooner rather than later, doncha know. Now isn't that something? Don't we all need friends like that." Clarence chuckled.

"Did Josie say this recently or a while ago?" said Osborne.

"Ah, she's been bragging off and on since school started in the fall. You know something else I noticed? Those girls are not friendly to each other. Makes me wonder how they can live in the same house."

"How do you mean 'not friendly'?" said Ray, opening another beer for Clarence.

"Just watching 'em get on the bus you can tell. Josie always sits up front—she's got two pals and they giggle and make fun of some of the other kids. But Frances is different. Very serious that one. Always goes to the back, always sits alone. Stares out the window most of the ride. She's got something on her mind if you ask me."

"Maybe she's wondering if she inherits a million," said Ray.

"Could be," said Clarence, finishing the first of his beers. "Could well be."

"You know a guy by the name of Jake Cahak by any chance?" said Osborne.

"Guy with a Minnesota plate—drives a Dodge RAM?"

"Yeah, you see him around much?"

"Can I tell you two something in private?" said Clarence. "You can't tell anyone or I'll be in big trouble."

"Cross my heart," said Ray.

"Strict confidence," said Osborne.

"That Josie slipped me a fifty-dollar bill to let her off early to meet that guy. I shouldn't be doing that." Clarence shrugged. Osborne knew fifty dollars was a lot to a man whose weekly take-home was maybe three hundred bucks.

"She met Jake?"

"Yep, he was always there waitin' for her."

"And Frances?"

"Oh, she hates that bastard. You should see the look on her face when he shows up. She never got off early. No sirree."

Ray's cell phone rang. He checked the number and handed it to Osborne. "Looks like it's the Chief, Doc. Why don't you take it?"

TWENTY-SIX

"Doc, where are you?"

"At the Birchwood Bar with Ray and a friend of his. You sound tense, Lew. What's wrong?"

"Had a call from Gina a few minutes ago. She's onto something serious. They've located the computer used to steal credit card numbers from people buying fishing licenses. Mildred's Food Shop."

"Lew..." Osborne was speechless.

"Whether or not Mildred was storing the credit card information and selling it remains to be seen. Could be the girls are involved, who knows at this point. Gina is meeting me at the shop in half an hour. I'm hoping— since you know Frances, Doc—that she might open up more easily if you're there."

"Do the girls know you're coming?"

"No and I don't want them to."

"Need Ray?"

"Since he's right there with you—wouldn't hurt. Ask him if he would walk the entire property. I know Jesperson did a rush job—plus those Wausau boys are worthless outdoors. They don't have the eye Ray has."

"Remember it was dark when they were there, Lew," said Osborne.

"You're right, I'm not being fair. Ask Ray to start as far outside Mildred's property as seems reasonable and work his way in."

"Okay, we're on our way," said Osborne, getting up from the barstool. "Any more news from the Wausau lab?"

"Only that Josie made dozens of calls to 'a boy named Jake Cahak.'"

"'A boy'?"

"Given her age, that's what they assumed. I'm not surprised. Gina found some strange files on Josie's laptop, too. Password protected. We'll get Josie to open those and let's hope that girl hasn't gotten herself into something nasty."

Clarence was disappointed they had to run off but Ray encouraged him to take the rest of his beers and go home. "A bus driver does not need a DUI," he said.

"Yep, you got that right," said Clarence as he followed them out the door. "Lose the pension, doncha know."

OSBORNE DROPPED RAY off at the far end of Mildred's block near an alley that led to the field behind the old barn. "Did I tell you I found Mildred's pet raccoon in the field back there? About fifty yards south of the barn. If Jesperson's people didn't find the carcass, I'm sure some eagle or fisher has. Watch out so you don't step in it."

"I'll keep an eye out," said Ray. "Been so unusually warm this fall the ground didn't freeze until a couple weeks ago. Who knows what I'll find. Good luck with the girls, Doc. Jeez, I sure as hell hope Mildred's death has nothing to do with them."

OSBORNE WAS SURPRISED to see the Open sign lit in the window of the store. Lew's cruiser and Gina's red rental car, a Jeep Liberty, were parked in the lot so he hurried inside. Stools had been pulled up on both sides of the counter. Gina sat behind the counter near the computer dedicated to fish and game licenses. While Lew was seated, too, she was in front of the cash register. Frances sat between the two women and Josie, her arms folded, leaned against the door to the sitting room Mildred had used to watch TV between customers.

"Have a seat, Doc," said Lew in a lighthearted tone. "We've been going over a few things with the girls here." She and Gina smiled at him and Osborne did his best to smile back as he took the stool next to the one that Josie was supposed to occupy.

"We just started chatting a few minutes ago," said Lew. "Frances is showing us how the license applications are handled from here. Go ahead, Frances."

"It's simple, really," said Frances. She proceeded to enter Gina's name, address and Social Security number as if she was applying for a fishing license. "Then I would submit your information to the state and within a minute or two we would receive a print-out that we then slip into one of these plastic covers. Very simple," said Frances with an easy smile—crooked but not pained. She was more relaxed and self-confident than Osborne had ever seen her. He was amazed at the transformation.

"And if I want to use my credit card?" said Gina.

"We run it through this machine," said Frances, pointing to a small black box with a digital readout sitting on the counter. "But for fishing and hunting licenses only—no using cards of any kind for groceries. Mrs. Taggert didn't take any credit cards until the state forced her to a couple years ago. She refused to buy a computerized cash register even. I guess you can say we're wireless but barely."

Osborne continued to be impressed with how composed Frances was. She was sitting up straight, her shoulders back and, as she spoke, she looked both Lew and Gina in the eye. Her voice was soft but firm with a natural grace that Osborne had never noticed: this was a new Frances Dark Sky.

"Do you recall the last time that Mildred would have upgraded the security and firewalls on this?" said Gina, waving at the licensing equipment on the counter.

"I doubt she ever did," said Frances. "Nothing has changed since it was installed. And she had no computers whatsoever when Josie and I moved in four years ago."

"Has it been that long?" said Osborne. "Gosh, Frances, seems like just yesterday you came for your first dental exam." Frances gave him a shy smile but didn't answer. "You know, girls, I've always kind of worried about you. Mildred was not…well, she didn't seem to be very pleasant at times."

"She was okay," said Frances. "She always made us a really nice breakfast—"

"Oh, sure, but she wouldn't let you wear your good jeans," said Josie. With a slight roll of the eyes, Frances ignored her sister.

"Her bark was worse than her bite, really," said Frances. "She was always nervous when customers were here. But pretty nice otherwise—to me, anyway."

"Yeah," said Josie in a snide tone, "easy for you to say. You were her pet."

Frances gave her sister a long look. "I wasn't her pet. I was the one willing to do my share around here." Josie shrugged. "Dr. Osborne," said Frances, "I know people think Mildred was mean to us but…" She paused for a second, her eyes on the counter.

She looked up, locking her eyes on Osborne's. "Do you have any idea what it's like living with someone, even if they're your mother, who is on drugs all the time? Cocaine, meth, ecstasy? With people coming through your home who are wiped out and weird. My life on the res was a nightmare—"

"Shut up!" shouted Josie from the corner. "That's not true. Mom was framed. She wasn't dealing and she didn't do drugs like you say. You're making all this up. Don't believe a word she says," said Josie jabbing a finger at Frances as she spoke.

"Girls…" said Lew.

"She has her reality and I have mine," said Frances, unruffled by her sister's outburst. "So, Josie, if you think Mom's so great why don't you want to move back to the res?" Before her sister could answer, Frances said, "Because we're safe here, Josie. Safe."

"Frances," said Gina, sounding anxious to change the subject, "we've got Josie's laptop but where's yours?"

"I don't have one," said Frances. "I work on one of the school's during study hall or the school will let us sign one out overnight. I'll do that this week 'cause I have a paper for my lit class due next Wednesday and I'll need it for that. Why?"

"Just wondering," said Gina.

"What about your cell phone?" said Lew.

"I don't have one of those either. Josie got her laptop and cell phone from Mrs. Reece. She paid for the service. Mildred couldn't afford cell phones plus—"

"Chief Ferris," said Josie, interrupting, "I was just wondering—do you know if Mr. Reece and Blue have read Mrs. Reece's will yet?"

"I don't know if they have," said Lew, "but Dr. Osborne and I met with her lawyer. We discussed the will—and I remember you said you heard Blue and her mother arguing over money, right? Could it have been over the will?"

"Maybe it was," said Josie. "I know Blue was very angry. Sounded like she was ready to hit her mother."

"You know, Josie," said Frances, "you really shouldn't say things like that unless you know something for sure."

"I know what I heard," said Josie with a defiant look. "What about Mrs. Reece's will? She left money to people, didn't she?"

"You mean like yourself?" asked Lew. Josie nodded.

"She may have intended to, Josie, but she died before she could rewrite a will that she signed several years ago."

Disbelief crossed Josie's face. "You mean she didn't leave me any money?"

"Not according to the lawyer," said Lew.

The room was very quiet. "I don't believe you," said Josie. "She promised me."

"Josie, Nolan Reece was an unusual woman," said Lew. "Over the last few days we've learned that she didn't always tell the truth—not even to her own family. She was not an emotionally healthy person. Now, that said it doesn't mean she didn't like—"

"Um…um." The girl covered her eyes with both hands. "Can I go to my room?"

"In the barn?" said Lew. Josie nodded. "Yes, but don't leave your room, Josie. We need to talk more. In fact, Gina, will you go with Josie, please? I'll be over shortly."

"Chief Ferris," said Frances when her sister was out the door, "I have something you should see." She opened a drawer next to the counter and pulled out a long white envelope across which had been written, "To be Opened After My Death."

"This morning, I thought I should open the store. Mrs. Taggert would have wanted that."

"Legally, you can't do that, Frances," said Lew. "The estate needs to be settled first."

"Oh…gee. Am I in trouble?"

"I suggest you close the shop until we know what is legal and what is not. And the envelope?"

"Mrs. Taggert told me last year when she was teaching me how to run the shop—you know, place orders, take care of the bookkeeping, all that stuff—she said if she got really sick or something happened, I should open this envelope that she kept at the bottom of the cash drawer. She said Mr. Craigemeier who did the taxes—he would have a copy, too. So I opened it last night."

She handed the envelope over and Lew read the contents. She looked up at Frances. "Do you think your sister had anything to do with Mildred's death?"

"I don't know. I...really, I don't know."

"You girls don't get along," said Lew.

Frances did not hesitate. "Get along? Get along? I hate Josie. She's a pathological liar, has been since we were little, and even though Mrs. Taggert did her best to be good to us in her way—Josie would sneak in here and steal money from the cash register. Then lie about it. She would say I did it."

MILDRED WAS NEVER one to waste words—in life or in death. Her letter was succinct:

To all concerned: I have arranged for my cremation and would like my ashes to be scattered somewhere around Loon Lake. Frances Dark Sky can
decide where that will be. Half of all my worldly
possessions, including my collection of raccoons,
my shop and my properties are to go to Frances
Dark Sky on one condition—she must graduate
from college. The remaining half of my estate is to
go to the Northwoods Wild Animal & Raptor
Rescue Center.

Not one penny goes to Josephine Dark Sky. She
stole her share from the till. I watched her do it.

Sincerely,
Mildred Rubado Taggert

IT WAS DATED and witnessed by a person whose name Osborne did not recognize. In parentheses beside the name, Mildred had scribbled: "a customer stopping by on their way to Eagle River."

TWENTY-SEVEN

ENTERING THE OLD barn through the door beside the empty raccoon cage, Osborne followed Lew toward a door off to the left, which led to the second floor. The ground level of the barn was everything he expected: dark and cobwebbed with Mildred's old Chevrolet parked in the back, boxes of canned foods and other shop supplies stacked along one wall, rusting tools leaning haphazardly in the corners. On opening the door, they discovered a freshly painted and renovated stairwell leading up to an expansive sitting area. Gina was on a sofa waiting for them.

"Doug Jesperson was right—this is amazing," said Lew, looking around the room. It was furnished with new, contemporary furniture. Osborne walked over to one of the windows. He noticed it was open a good two inches, which didn't surprise him. The room was quite nice but stuffy with the smell of fresh paint. "Brand-new windows, brand-new screens, even the sash," he said. "Who would think this was here?" A small kitchen area anchored one end of the room and another door opened to a white-tiled bathroom.

Across the room, a door stood open to an empty but tastefully furnished bedroom while another door was closed. "Josie's room," said Gina, answering their questioning looks. "She said Mrs. Reece paid for all this but Mildred wouldn't let her change the lower level because she was afraid her taxes would go up."

"Frances told us she refuses to stay out here because it's Josie's," said Lew. "And because it was easier for her to help Mildred if she slept in the main house."

"Let me knock on the door and get Josie out here," said Lew. "She's got a few questions to answer still."

"Let's wait a few minutes," said Gina. "I've got something to show you first. I set up Josie's laptop over there," she said, pointing to a table near one of the windows. "Doc, Chief, I'm not sure how much you know about data transmission—"

"Very little," said Osborne.

"Me, neither," said Lew. "I share a tech guy with the sheriff's department and depend on him when our system goes down."

"Well, this unit with the flashing lights is a router," said Gina. "It allows Josie's laptop to go on the Internet wireless. But what we have over here is highly unusual."

She pointed to a small antenna, telescope-shaped, beside the router that had one wire running into the open computer and another plugged into an electrical outlet. "This is an antenna that I'm betting the crime lab assumed was used for satellite television or radio. In fact, it's identical to antennas we've seen that are designed to hoover data out of the air."

"What do you mean exactly?" said Lew.

"I mean that someone could, if they knew the password of the person transmitting data from the shop—

whether credit card or license information—access that direct from the radio waves carrying the data."

"No," said Lew, "I thought there were security systems to prevent that?"

"There are now but a lot of small merchants still use the original encoding systems and those have been cracked so often by hackers it isn't funny. My students researched a data theft that occurred in Minneapolis where over forty million credit cards were compromised using exactly this kind of antenna, which is capable of intercepting streaming data."

"Josie," said Lew, walking over to knock loudly on the bedroom door. "Please come out here." The girl opened the door, her face sullen and tear-stained.

"What now?" she said.

"Josie, sit down with me and let's go over a few files you've got on your laptop here," said Gina, attempting to sound friendly. The girl flounced across the room and plunked herself into a chair at the table.

"What's this?" said Gina.

"Dunno, that's not mine."

"Oh, is this something Frances was working on?"

"No."

"And this?"

"I have no idea—those are Jake's folders."

"You mean Jake uses your laptop? Doesn't he have his own computer?"

"He does but he likes mine."

"Well, okay, Josie—would you please open these folders for us?" Josie leaned forward and hit a few keys only to sit back and throw her hands up.

"I can't. I don't know his password."

"Okay, then. We'll have to find Jake, I guess." Gina was determinedly cheery. "And I'll hold on to the laptop until we can reach him."

"No doubt he's at the Reeces'," said Osborne. "We can find him there."

MINUTES LATER, STANDING outside the barn in the parking area near Gina's rental car, Lew said, "So Gina, you sure you're up to working out at your cabin? I worry that you're warm enough out there. That point where the Gudegast feeds into Loon Lake can get pretty darn breezy. We're due for a winter storm tonight with winds up to forty miles an hour. Doc, here, has an extra bedroom."

"So does Ray," said Gina with a guilty grin. "No, I'm fine plus I have wireless access out there, which I need. My big problem is no cell phone service. Now tell me— how is it I can get wireless Internet access through the cable company but no cell phone service? Sheesh! At least I have a landline and, hopefully, the phone company will have turned it on by the time I get out there today. I called them two days ago and they promised."

"I'm not sure I have that number," said Lew.

"It's in the latest edition of your Loon Lake phone book under Gina Palmer but I'll call you when I get there. My plan is to get in touch with one of my grad students whose hacking skills you wouldn't believe. He'll be able to crack the encryption on those files for me. I sure as hell would like to see those before alerting this Jake character."

"Hey, guys," said Ray, loping up the drive alongside Mildred's house. "Sorry to take so long but I was… accosted by one of the neighbors out in the field back there who thought I was lurking…and made an offer…to change my life with his baseball bat."

"No, Ray—where is this person?" Lew started forward.

"Not to worry, Chief, I assured him I was your deputy. When he calmed down, he had some interesting info for us. Seems he's been watching a green Dodge RAM drive through the back doors to park in the old barn here almost every night and quite often during the day. He didn't think much about it until Mildred's death. As far as he knows—and I do believe he's one of those gentlemen who knows the business of all his neighbors—the truck hasn't been here since."

"Ah," said Lew. "So Jake and Josie have broken up, have they?"

"More likely he hasn't been here because the girls were staying elsewhere and the shop's not been open," said Gina.

Ray glanced up over Osborne's head and waved at the open window. "Hi, there, Josie. How're ya doin?"

The girl didn't answer. She slammed the window shut and disappeared.

TWENTY-EIGHT

"MIKE OL' BOY—life doesn't get much better than this," said Osborne as he lounged in his easy chair with the wool plaid blanket from Father's Day across his lap. He had on his favorite slippers and the ottoman tucked under his legs just right. The logs in the fireplace crackled and spit as they burned and Mike, curled up on his round sheepskin bed, snored away. Ice pelted the windows, but man and dog were warm and cozy.

After sending Gina off with Josie's laptop computer, Lew had let Osborne know she planned to put in a good three hours on paperwork before heading out to her place—hopefully ahead of the snowstorm. He'd offered to cook dinner—takeout pizza—but she had declined with a swift kiss and a squeeze of his arm.

"I have got to catch up on my sleep, Doc—may I take a rain check?" And so he had picked up a small pizza for himself, which was now baking in the oven, and settled in to enjoy the solitude. He started to page through the first of three fly fishing catalogs that he had been saving: time to decide what to buy Lewellyn Ferris for Christmas. Certainly something other than panty hose.

Turning the pages, he grew perplexed. To the best

of his knowledge, she owned every piece of fly fishing
gear that caught his eye. Then he saw something
intriguing. Given the need to travel by horseback out
in Jackson Hole, what about an Orvis "Safe Passage
Complete Chest Pack"? The catalog described a rear
backpack with room for a poncho or a jacket and
lunch—and a front pack similar to a fly fishing vest.
Now that could be terrific for the ride. He knew Lew
was concerned about trusting all her best fishing gear
to a pack mule. He marked the page.

A blast of wind against the windows and the chat-
tering of ice reminded him it might be wise to bring in
a few extra logs before the weather got worse. He
decided to flip through a few more pages before moving—it was just too comfortable sitting where he was
at the moment.

He opened to a page of trout flies designed to lure
salmon and steelhead with their gaudy colors and large
hooks. A slash of purple tipped black with a big red
eye caught his attention. The description of the leech-
like trout fly said the Hot Shot was guaranteed to
"writhe in the water like a crippled lamprey." Wasn't a
Hot Shot the lure that Nolan Reece had insisted Ray
use that last day that he had been willing to guide her?
No wonder he had felt so frustrated by the woman—
Northwoods lakes don't have salmon and steelhead.
What was she thinking?

Osborne snorted. That's right—now he remembered. Ray had said Nolan Reece was one of those
Illinois transplants who have so little sense of why a
fish takes a bait that they think it makes sense to match

the color of their lures to the color of their boats—as if fish recognize a fashion statement. Is there a blue Hot Shot or was Ray exaggerating? After all, that fancy bassboat in the Reeces' shore station was not purple—it was blue.

It was blue. Osborne started up in his chair. He reached for the cordless phone on the table beside him and dialed. "Ray—what are you doing?"

The sleepy voice on the other end of the line said, "Napping, which is exactly what you should be doing, Doc. Snowstorm biorhythms, doncha know."

"I'm going to swing by and pick you up in five minutes," said Osborne. "The Wausau boys told Lew that Nolan Reece had slivers of blue marine paint beneath her fingernails. I just remembered that boat in the shore station beside their dock—the one near the pontoon? It's blue."

"You're right," said Ray, more alert. "See ya in a minute."

DURING THE SHORT time he was parked in front of Ray's trailer, waiting for him to pull on some warm clothes, ice began to coat his car. He had to turn up the defroster and chip away until the ice fractured in thin sheets and slid down the windshield. He honked, hoping Ray would hurry so they could get to the Reeces' before that long driveway of theirs turned into a toboggan chute.

At last Ray appeared and none too soon for conditions. They drove into a deepening dusk where dense fog had knit acres of barren aspen into a soft gray afghan, the hills defined only as folds of black.

Nestled against that blackness, the Reece house glowed like a holiday lantern. Andy came to the kitchen door within seconds of their knocking, both dogs barking behind him.

"Blue's not here," he said, "she's at her AA meeting with her friend from up the road—I'm hoping they get back any minute. The roads have to be treacherous."

"We're not here to see Blue," said Osborne.

"Oh, dammit!" said Andy. "You need me right now? I'm smack in the middle of a fantasy fishing challenge that could win me five million bucks."

"Five million for sitting in a chair in front of your computer? I can't believe it," said Ray. "Am I in the wrong boat or what—man!"

"You gotta get into this stuff, Ray," said Andy. "See, right now, if you register before December twenty-first and pick the top seven anglers of any tournament—"

"Andy, can we discuss this later?" said Osborne. "Ray and I stopped in to check your boats one last time. The crime lab needs a few details. Do you mind?"

"Oh, no," said Andy. "Help yourself. Here—" he hit a switch on the wall of the mudroom by the back door "—that's the light for the boathouse and you can turn more on when you get down there. I had Jake winterize and hang the boats this morning—just in time, too. Go right ahead."

OSBORNE AND RAY made it down the icy stairs to the boathouse without slipping and falling, though Osborne wasn't sure how. The boathouse was well-lit plus they both had heavy-duty flashlights. Given the good light and the fact the boats were suspended on chains from the boathouse rafters, it was easy to examine the undersides of each.

They headed straight for the glittering blue bassboat. Ray ran a beam of light across the exposed hull, which had the classic V-bottom with a flat pad running along the length of the boat, a feature designed to increase speed. At a point mid-center of the hull, the pad was marred with deep scratches. "Whoa," said Ray, "if I didn't know better, I'd say some animal had been clawing at this…"

"An animal named Nolan Reece," said Osborne in a grim tone. He held out an evidence bag while Ray used the tweezers on his pocketknife to remove slivers of paint from the scratched area on the hull.

"I better call Lew," said Osborne when they were done.

"Tonight? What can she do about this tonight, Doc? She looked so tired this afternoon. You sure this can't wait until tomorrow?"

"She'll want to know—"

Ray's cell phone rang. He checked the number and handed the phone to Osborne, saying, "You better start carrying your own goddamn phone, Doc. You get more calls on mine than I do."

TWENTY-NINE

"I was on the phone with Gina when she said someone was at her door," said Lew, her voice tense. "She said she'd call me right back. But she hasn't, Doc. I've tried back half a dozen times but the phone just rings busy. I know she doesn't have dial-up Internet so it can't be she's online. Thinking she might be on a call with one of her students, I had an operator try an emergency interrupt but she reported no one on the line.

"Couldn't tell me more than that. The phone company's repair service has a recorded message saying they're having trouble on the lines in the region due to weather so it sounds like it'll be awhile before they can get out to Gina's and see what the problem is. I'm very concerned."

"Gee, Lew," said Osborne, "with the ice buildup on the tree branches, I'll bet the phone wires came down. That's a landline phone she has at her place, isn't it?"

"You could be right. They've reported power lines down in Tomahawk. What worries me though is who was at the door? It's not like Gina lives here year 'round and has friends who drop in. Except for you and Ray, I doubt she even knows her neighbors. And with this weather, most people are hunkered down inside. If Ray is with you, who could it be that was at her door?"

"Where are you right now, Lew?"

"I'm still in town. I've been so worried I haven't left the department yet. Where are you two?"

"At the Reeces'. I was thinking about those scrapings under Nolan Reece's fingernails and remembered that one of the boats docked over here was blue—that big bassboat. Ray helped me get some paint scrapings off the hull pad, which, by the way, is badly scratched. Could be rocks or..."

"Let's deal with that later," said Lew. "Tell you what—I'm going to drive over to her place and make sure she's okay but I'd feel a heck of a lot better if I had back-up. Can't use Todd or Roger—one's handling a rollover on Highway 17 and the other a fender bender in the parking lot at the Loon Lake Market."

"We're heading back to my place right now," said Osborne, waving Ray towards the entrance to the boathouse. "Meet you there but take your time—the roads are icy and getting worse by the minute."

"I'm well aware of that."

Osborne handed the cell phone back to Ray. "Gina's not answering her cabin phone—"

"It's the ice," said Ray. "Bet you we lose service, too."

"Well, they were talking on the phone when Gina heard someone at her door and said she'd call back but Lew hasn't heard from her since. Lew's tried calling but all she gets is a busy signal. She got an operator to try to break into the call but the operator said no one was on the line. Lew tried the phone company repair service and got a recorded message."

"I still think it's ice," said Ray, "but worth checking out if it helps everyone relax. Given her place is on that point and exposed on three sides, we'll know the minute we drive in if she's alone or not."

"Unless they walked over."

"On this ice?" said Ray. "I doubt that."

LEW'S CRUISER WAS in Osborne's driveway when they got back. She had let herself into the house and was standing in the kitchen. She turned as they entered. "I tried calling out on your phone, Doc. This line's not down. You guys ready to go?"

"Take it easy, Chief," said Ray. "I'm sure there's an easy answer—"

"I hope you're right but…Gina had called to say her student was able to crack the passwords protecting those files," said Lew. "The files are full of personal credit card data. Now whether it's Josie or Jake we don't know, but one of the two has been siphoning the credit card numbers stored off the computer in Mildred's shop.

"Gina was in the midst of telling me that she has her students checking the contents of the laptop's files against the database they have of stolen cards when whoever it was knocked on her door. What if Jake Cahak learned from Josie that Gina has possession of that computer…"

"I hear you," said Ray. "Let's drive down in my truck as if I'm picking Gina up for dinner—which I am supposed to do, but not for another hour. The road into her place has a turnaround where we can check to see if any other cars are there—without our being seen. Okay with that?"

Lew nodded. "Let's hurry."

RAY BUMPED DOWN the drive that was quickly disappearing under the snow and yanked the wheel sharp to the left behind a dense stand of young balsam whose branches were beginning to droop from the weight of ice under a thickening blanket of fat, heavy snowflakes. It was less a turnaround than just enough space to pull in, back out and reverse without being seen from the cabin's porch, which was several hundred yards away.

"Wait," said Ray as Osborne started to push on the truck's door. "No one's wearing blaze orange, right?" They checked one another out. No bright colors—they'd blend.

Osborne heaved a shoulder at the passenger-side door, wishing for the umpteenth time that Ray might discover the miracle of silicon spray. After three attempts, the door opened at last with only the slightest creak. Since the other door had been frozen shut for as long as Osborne had known Ray, all three got out on the passenger side. To minimize noise, Ray, the last one out, left the engine running and the door ajar.

"Be very careful," cautioned Osborne in a whisper as they moved forward, "it's glare ice under this snow. Please, don't anyone fall and break a bone."

Just as they crept up behind the balsams, the door to the screened-in porch banged open. Windows from the interior of the cabin threw enough light for them to see

Jake Cahak step down two stairs, a rifle in both hands as he swung to the left, then to the right.

"Damn, he's got an AR-15," said Ray, voice low.

"I don't see anybody," shouted Jake back to someone inside. "Enough snow out here I'd see tracks if there was. You're hearing things. Probably just a car going down the road. Hey, ask that woman how much longer for those damn files to load. This snow's turning into a blizzard. I want outta here, pronto."

A female voice from inside hollered back, "Twenty minutes she says. Thirty at the most."

"Josie!" Lew and Osborne whispered simultaneously.

"Shit," said Jake, swinging from one side to another once more before stepping back inside the door. He lingered on the porch, a dark figure barely discernable against the wood paneling.

Whispering, Ray put out a hand to restrain Lew, who had pulled her Sig Sauer from its holster. "Don't even think about it, Chief. That's a black rifle he's got. Comes with a magnifier on the scope that will make you look like you're two feet away."

"But we're in the dark—and he's got light behind him—"

"And a flashlight attached to the barrel that won't shatter when he fires. Against that gun of his, yours is no match. Whatever you do, don't shoot. Let's think about this—"

"We better think fast," said Osborne. "Sounds like all we have is fifteen or twenty minutes to figure it out."

The three of them stood in the darkness, the only sound their breathing as they studied the outside of the cabin. Snow continued to fall—fat, heavy flakes softening the outlines of the small building.

"Maybe there's a deer trail off to one side that I could follow in toward—"

"No," Lew cut Ray off with a harsh whisper, "not in this snow—no way to hide your tracks. And with the ice, you're likely to slip and fall, and then what? Doc, Ray—I don't think we can get there from here without being seen.

"If I call for back-up, that's at least a half hour before someone gets here given the hazardous road conditions and other emergency calls. If we confront Jake, I worry that we risk Gina's life not to mention our own lives—and Josie's. Dammit! Why did Gina have to buy a place so exposed anyway?"

Even as she spoke the snowfall lightened momentarily, throwing the cabin into sharp relief with only the trees behind it—lakeside—offering any cover.

"I know," said Ray. "Let's circle 'round and come in from the back across the channel. Chances are there's maybe fifty feet of open water, we can pull on shore and stay behind the trees that run along the lot line up to the cabin. We'll come in the back way and surprise them."

"It's an option, but who's got a boat?" asked Lew.

"Mine's trailered and ready to go," said Ray. "I was planning to drop it off at the storage locker before picking up Gina. Take me two seconds to hitch up the trailer and we'll circle 'round easily on a logging trail that crosses the Gudegast just north of Gina's place."

Lew looked first at Osborne, then at Ray. She made

up her mind: "Okay, but let's move fast and hope that whatever Gina's doing, she takes her time."

RAY BENT DOWN, struggling to get the trailer hitched as fast as possible. In his rush he slipped, sliding feet first under the back of his truck and landing hard on his back.

"Oh, gosh, are you okay?" asked Lew as she and Doc grabbed both arms to pull him out and up.

"Yeah. I'll feel it in the morning but I'm fine." With a few quick swipes, Ray brushed the snow off his butt, then hooked the chain onto the trailer hitch and motioned for them to get back in the pick-up. It was snowing so heavily now that they were driving in whiteout conditions, barely able to see more than twenty feet, if that, ahead.

Ray pulled the truck and trailer onto Loon Lake Road heading east to the stop sign where, wheels spinning, he swung onto the county highway. He continued over a bridge then skidded through a left turn onto a town road that appeared to come to a dead end. But an opening between two tall Norway spruces turned out to be a rough logging lane.

"Only Ray could find this," muttered Lew as if questioning her decision to try the back way. The truck banged along until they reached a dirt-covered culvert that served as a bridge. Just past that was a clearing with a portable sawmill, its stack of uncut logs and fresh-hewn planks wrapped in tarps. Ray kept going.

He pulled to a stop behind tag alders lining the shore. The snowfall was so heavy they could barely make out the lights of Gina's cabin across the way. But the trees were there—the border of mature shrubs that Ray had promised ran like tall soldiers along one side of her place. Osborne noticed the ice on the channel extended a good fifteen feet, then thirty feet or more of open water all the way to the opposite shore, thanks to the current from the Gudegast. He was relieved. The open water was what they needed to cross in just a moment or two.

He and Lew got out of the truck so Ray could back it around and drop the boat trailer onto the ice along their side of the channel. He moved fast to slide the boat off the trailer and, with help from both Osborne and Lew, scoot it over the ice until the stern broke through. Thinking it had dropped into water, Ray gave one more shove. It went nowhere.

"What the hell?" he walked over the ice, his boots breaking through to hit sand. "Oh no," he said. "The water is so low, the boat's still on sand." The three of them pushed again but the boat budged barely an inch.

"Maybe we can walk across?" said Osborne. "We're wearing boots." Even as he mentioned the boots, he was sorry he was wearing gloves and not mitts. His hands were freezing. Lew grabbed a moment to zip her parka so that the collar and hood left only her nose and eyes exposed. The wind was strong from the north, biting their faces.

"Sorry, Doc, even with low water there's a drop-off of nearly ten feet right through the center there," said Ray. "But I got an idea—just wait." He ran back to the truck, slid across to the driver's seat and drove off, the trailer clattering along behind him.

Lew looked at Osborne and shook her head. "Another

idea? What is that man up to? I am so worried. Doc, we ran out of time ten minutes ago."

The defeat on her face was more than Osborne could bear. He pulled her to him and wrapped his arms around her, held her for a long moment. "Don't give up yet," he said into her hair. "Ray's not stupid."

Lew stepped away, clapping her gloved hands together to keep them warm. "I know. It's just…this seems impossible—" Just as she checked her watch for the tenth time they heard the clatter of the trailer before they saw the truck. Ray hit the brakes and jumped out saying, "Hey, you two, grab those logs and let's roll 'em out over the sand. But first, help me yank this boat back onto the ice."

HE HAD THROWN half a dozen logs, five feet long, into the bed of the truck. He grabbed one, Lew and Osborne another and they rushed across the ice to lay the logs parallel and horizontal to the shoreline. Back and forth they ran until the log surface extended the extra feet needed to get past the sand. Pulling the boat sideways, they pushed it stern-first over the logs, which were as slick as the ice. This time the boat dropped into water.

"Get ready," said Ray, as they all three clambered into the boat. He had the oars moving before Osborne had both feet in and it seemed like less than thirty seconds before they were bumping against the far shore. Boat pulled up, they paused to listen. Voices could be heard from inside the cabin. They started forward, Ray in the lead.

THIRTY

SCRAMBLING UP THE bank from the shoreline was not as easy as it appeared. A layer of ice beneath what was now two inches of wet snow made each step forward seem like two steps back. Osborne wasn't the only one whose boots kept slipping. Nor did things improve when the three of them reached the screen of arbor vitae running along Gina's property line: the trees—though a good six feet high and densely branched—had gaps of three to four feet between them.

"Stay low," whispered Ray, who had taken the lead. Osborne did the best he could as he crouched behind Lew. It worried him that the snow had suddenly stopped and a break in the cloud cover turned the rising moon into a floodlight exposing the cabin in its snowy clearing. Any approach would leave tracks visible from inside.

The unmistakable crack of a rifle shot caused Osborne to freeze for a second before slamming himself into the snow behind Lew and Ray. Was that from inside the cabin? Or outside? It happened so fast he couldn't tell. He held his breath. Lew and Ray were motionless. Thank goodness the clumps of grass between the trees are high, thought Osborne, decent cover. More shots and the sound of bullets thudding into the trunks of the arbor vitae.

"Josie, someone's here," cried a hoarse male voice from near the cabin. "Grab that laptop and get in the truck! Go! Go! Go!"

"Godammit," said Lew under her breath as she inched forward in a belly-crawl. Ray was moving, too. Osborne hesitated and was relieved when they stopped. A low rise between the line of trees and the cabin would be difficult to cross without being seen. The windows at the rear of the cabin were lit and the curtains pulled back. Anyone who crossed that clearing was a target.

The sound of a door slamming, an engine revving and the spinning of tires on gravel encouraged Ray, who jumped to his feet and ran straight for the lighted window. He peered in, then turned and waved Osborne and Lew forward. "I don't see anyone," he said in a low voice when they reached him. "All you can see is the kitchen and it's empty. Let's hope they haven't taken Gina hostage." He tried the back door but it was locked. He banged on it. A wait. He banged again. When nothing happened dread hit Osborne in the gut. Another crunch of tires from the other side of the cabin…then silence.

Pulling her Sig Sauer pistol from its holster, Lew said, "Ray, maybe we should try the front—"

The door flew open and Gina stood there: a silhouette against the bright lights of the kitchen. "Oh, thank God," she said, stepping back and holding the door open. "They just left and…and I'm okay, I'm okay." Her eyes widened as she resisted breaking down, but her shoulders drooped and her voice cracked as she tried to smile. "You don't know how good it is to see you guys—if I'd known you were coming I'd have baked a cake." By the last word she was in tears. "I hate crying," she sobbed. "I'm just fine." Ray gathered her into his arms, patting her back as she wept.

"GINA, TAKE YOUR time, we're not going anywhere," said Lew as Osborne got Gina a glass of water and Ray eased her into a chair at the kitchen table.

"But don't you—they're heading for Canada," said Gina, rising in her seat. "Josie told me her friend killed those women. Someone needs to—"

"Settle down, kiddo," said Lew. "I'm about to alert all law enforcement in the region. They can take it from here." Gina sat back, wiping at her face with a Kleenex that Ray had handed her, then took several deep breaths while Lew punched in the emergency number for the switchboard on the cabin phone. "Working fine," she said with a faint grin as she held the receiver high.

Two seconds later Lew was instructing Marlene to put out an APB for Jake Cahak's Dodge RAM. "We have reason to think they're headed for Canada," she said. "Tell Wisconsin, Michigan and Minnesota authorities I suggest they cover every possible route between here and the border. But I want southern routes covered as well just in case they decide to pull a fast one and head for Illinois. And, please, Marlene, be sure to repeat that these two people are armed and dangerous and one or both are wanted for murder."

After giving brief physical descriptions of Jake and Josie, she hung up, pulled out a chair and sat down at the kitchen table. "With luck, they'll be spotted within the hour. Gina, feeling better?" Gina nodded with a faint smile.

Lew pulled out her notepad. "I need you to start at the beginning and tell us exactly what happened. Every detail. Doc, would you take notes, please? I don't have a tape recorder so I'll need yours for back-up. Ray, you're in charge of the coffee."

"Got it," said Ray, jumping up from the table.

"JOSIE HEARD US talking in the parking lot at Mildred's place," said Gina. "That's how she and Jake knew where to find me. They were desperate for her laptop. Those files I found were full of data that he hadn't yet forwarded to the connection up in Montreal that's been buying it from him.

"That's who knocked on the door when—thinking it was Ray—I said I'd call you back. But they barged right in before I could. He had a very unpleasant-look-ing gun and Josie was right behind him. He spotted my computer open on the desk in the front room and grabbed for it. He was unplugging it when I suggested that he might want to be sure he could open the files before leaving.

"Don't ask me how," Gina raised both hands as if still surprised at herself, "but I managed to stay pretty calm. Kinda like 'oh, hey, people barge in here every day, go right ahead, take what you like.' I stayed cool. Even when the phone rang—"

"That had to be me," said Lew.

"That's what I figured. Worried that any calls might make the situation worse, I took the phone off the hook. Sorry."

"Hey, that's what got us out here," said Lew. "Thank goodness you were able to stall 'em."

"Maybe 'cause I was calm, Jake decided to sit down and try to open the files—which, of course, he couldn't. I explained—excuse me, I lied—and said that I had already e-mailed the files to a tech in Chicago who'd hacked into them and who was in the process of sending the files back to me under new encryption so I could analyze the data. I was honest—I said we were looking for who had been stealing credit card numbers.

"That's when Jake threatened me. He said if I didn't open the files for him... That's the one time I was really afraid because he became so enraged so fast I wasn't sure I could reason with him. But Josie calmed him down and I offered to help out. If they wouldn't hurt me, I said, I would give them the new password. Meantime the files were still loading so they knew they would have to wait for that to finish."

"And they believed you?" said Lew.

"Yeah. Jake could see it happening on the screen. What was lucky for me is he's got system skills but the guy's no hacker. He knew he couldn't get past an encrypted file without help."

"If that's the case, how did they get into Mildred's data in the first place?" said Lew. "Wouldn't that have required a password?"

"Yes. And what do you think that was? Aside from

the fact that she kept an index card in the cash register with the damn password written on it..."

"Wait," said Ray, turning around from where he was spooning coffee into Gina's coffeemaker, "let me guess—raccoon?"

"Close, try again."

Ray tipped his head, thinking hard, then said, "Raccoon polka?"

"No," said Gina laughing as color crept back into her face, 'babyraccoon.' One word, all lower case.

"By now I've convinced them that the files they need are loading into the laptop on the desk and since they have to wait, I'm hoping I can keep them here until Ray comes to pick me up for dinner."

"An hour?" said Lew. "You were going to keep them waiting an hour?"

"When was the last time you worked with a huge file, Chief? Those can take a long time to load. I was afraid that if I gave them the computer, I'd be the next person with a bullet in my head. I was desperate to buy time."

"Were you really loading files?" said Osborne.

"Oh, yes," said Gina. "Definitely loading files. Couldn't fudge that. So while we're waiting, I offered them a deal. I said I was a private contractor, that I had been stiffed by a couple of the banks that had hired me and if they were interested I could provide more credit card data on one condition—they had to cut me in on the profits. I made it a point to ask for a lot—thirty percent.

"But I also said they would have to let me set up a system that would hide what was happening. I think that's what convinced Jake I was for real because then he opened up and told me how he works. Installing state of the art computer systems in expensive homes has made him an expert on computer security from spam filters to firewalls—and where the gaps are. So he jumped on this because he knew right away that I knew what I was talking about."

"Gina, this took guts," said Osborne. "I'm not sure I would have the fortitude."

"Doc, you're looking at someone who, in my years as an investigative reporter, had to sneak up on mobsters' garages to steal their garbage. You want scary? That's scary. This was unsettling, but Jake and Josie were so nervous about getting that computer and all the files that they had to trust me. Jake may be able to siphon data but, like I said, he's no hacker."

"So now you've got business partners," said Lew, "and you've got them on hold. How long were they here? More than an hour?"

"No, just an hour or so. But it didn't take long for Jake to get so anxious that Josie sent him outside to keep watch. While he was patrolling the cabin, she double-crossed the guy and offered me a better deal."

"Are you serious?" said Lew. "Girl's got guts."

"Oh, yes, chatty Cathy's got it all figured out. She offered to go partners with me fifty-fifty because she's already planning to dump Jake once she meets his connection. Said his quick temper makes him high risk. I asked her what she meant by that. She thought it over then told me he's killed two people and she does not intend to take the rap as an accomplice."

"She told you all this?" said Lew, astounded.

"It was just me and her here for half an hour—and she did all the talking. The girl's a schemer and I can tell she's managed to fool a lot of people. Her mistake is thinking she's smarter than everyone else."

"Don't they always," said Lew with a shake of her head. "Go on. Was she specific as to who he killed? Anything about Nolan Reece?"

"I took a chance and asked if Jake had anything to do with that. He sure did. Josie said he was furious at the way Nolan had screamed at him in front of all the people here preparing for the engagement party. That wasn't the first time she'd gone after him, either. He despised the woman.

"Plus he was under the impression that Josie was in her will and could inherit a hefty chunk of money. He knew Nolan always went down to the dock late at night so he planned ahead—lowering the fishing boat and waiting in the woods near the dock.

"Josie said he hit her with a club so hard she blacked out and fell into the lake—"

"Which explains why we found Nolan's bridge on the other side of the dock, Lew," said Osborne, interrupting. "She was hit so hard that the bridge flew out of her mouth and across the dock to where you found it."

Lew nodded. "What else did Josie say, Gina?"

"Before Nolan came to, Jake pulled the boat over on top of her so she couldn't move and sat in the boat until he knew she was dead, then hoisted the boat back onto its shore station.

"It was on Thanksgiving after he had driven the girls back to Mildred's and was hanging out in the barn with Josie that he bragged about how it was the perfect crime—totally unaware that Mildred had entered the barn to search for her missing pet. Mildred saw Jake's truck parked there. Standing on the stairs she overheard Jake and confronted the two of them. She shouted at him to get out, that she was going to call the police and started back towards the shop. He ran down the stairs, grabbed his rifle from the back of the truck and shot her as she was crossing the parking lot."

"So it's all Jake," said Lew.

"Yes, it's all Jake."

"Poor Mildred," said Osborne, "she was so heavy, so arthritic, she moved so slow. He must have had all the time in the world—"

"And shit for brains to leave those spent casings on the ground like that," said Ray.

"Probably didn't occur to him that shooting humans is different from bringing down an eight-point buck," said Osborne. "You need to pick up after yourself."

"Gina, are you saying that they left here with that computer and all those files?" said Lew. "This worries me. Although you did say one of your tech grad students downloaded those so we'll be able to notify the banks—"

"Let me show you something," said Gina with a smug look on her face. She marched across the kitchen and into the next room, past the desk to the door to her bedroom. "Look." She opened the door. On the nightstand near the bed was a white laptop.

"Josie has an Apple laptop and I have an Apple laptop. Same model. The one they grabbed is mine. The files that were loading were photos from my niece's wedding last month. This," said Gina, holding the flat white laptop high in triumph, "this is Josie's laptop with the data files.

"And everything on my laptop is backed up, so if I never see it again—no loss."

Before anyone could say more, the cabin phone rang. Gina picked it up, answered and said, "For you, Chief."

Lew took the phone, listened and said, "Thanks, Marlene." She set the phone back in its cradle and studied the floor for a moment before looking up to say, "A motorist just called in an accident on his cell phone. He's at the site of a green pick-up overturned on Highway 45 near Land o'Lakes, license plate BIG DOG.

"Ice and heavy slush on the roads up there—must have spun out. Two victims. The sheriff's deputies and ambulances are on their way."

JOSIE DARK SKY was thrown from the vehicle as it rolled, only to have it land on her. She was dead when the first squad car arrived. Jake, not wearing a seat belt, was still trapped in the rear of the extended cab when the vehicle caught fire. He died on the way to the hospital. Gina's laptop computer was found in a pile of brush heaped beside the highway—undamaged.

Arriving home to a charred pizza hours later that night, Osborne was less distracted by the sorry state of his dinner than by Ray Pradt's parting remark: "Wish we could've heard Jake's side of the story."

THIRTY-ONE

"THOSE BITS OF yarn that Ray found snagged on branches in the wooded area along the western edge of your property? They match the wool sweater Jake was wearing when he was killed," said Lew, reviewing her notes as she and Osborne met with Andy and Blue Reece in Lew's office.

It was late Tuesday afternoon and the preliminary report from the Wausau Crime Lab had arrived earlier that morning. "The lab was able to match those fibers easily as well as the paint scrapings from under your wife's fingernails. They came from the hull of the blue bassboat." Lew glanced over at Andy. "You may want to have that boat repainted—"

"I'm selling it," said Andy, his voice brusque with emotion. Whatever his feelings had been towards his late wife before her death, Andy had kept them to himself throughout the investigation. A class act in Osborne's view.

"Also, the rubber gloves that were found hidden with the two-by-four that was used in the assault contained skin cells that are being checked for DNA. It'll be a few weeks until we have confirmation on that— DNA testing takes a while. But I expect a match to Jake

Cahak. Just like the spent casings from the .223-caliber bullets found near the barn where Mildred Taggert was killed are used in black rifles like the one we found in his truck."

"And those match, too?" said Andy.

"Again, the ballistics testing has yet to be completed but I'm sure we'll see a match," said Lew. "I'll see that you get a copy of the final report on both investigations."

"Thank you," said Blue, "it helps us get past all this. The knowing, I mean."

"I understand," said Lew. "Every detail helps. When do you drive south?"

"We leave in the morning. Until today, the roads have been pretty bad."

"You're right about that," said Osborne. "My daughter and her family saw cars in the ditch and overturned semi-trailers as they drove back from Milwaukee Monday morning. You've been wise to wait."

EIGHTEEN INCHES OF snow had fallen since Saturday afternoon and Jake Cahak had not been the only person to drive too fast for conditions. The Loon Lake Police Department and the county sheriff's office had had two more fatal accidents to deal with before the storm passed. It was weather, too, that delayed the Murphys' trip north—though once they learned that Lew had no need to interrogate either of the parents or Barry, their trip was canceled.

Nolan Reece's body would be released to her husband and daughter that afternoon. Following Nolan's wishes, they had arranged with a local funeral home for cremation followed by a memorial service in Lake Forest and a final resting place in Loon Lake.

"My wife was difficult but she had her virtues," said Andy, rumbling in his baritone after Lew's closing of her notebook signaled the formalities were over. "She had a distinctive, original talent for design—one look at our house and you can see that. I think back to the woman I knew when we were young—if only her family had encouraged her to study architecture ... if only I had known how to make her happy." He studied the hands he held clasped tight in his lap. "I did my best to keep the promise that I made to her father and ... and yet—" he raised his deep, dark eyes "—it might have been better if we had divorced ... you know? She might be alive today."

"Mother's mental and emotional landscape was beyond our control, Andy," said Blue. "I think we did our best." Blue patted his hand.

"We met with Mom's lawyer this morning," she said, "and my trust comes under my control in two months. On my birthday—so there will be some changes made soon. Good changes." She smiled.

"Congratulations," said Osborne.

"Yes, first things first," said Blue, "Barry and I have decided to call off our engagement. Without my mom around to hassle us, his mother is being a little more understanding."

"What about his father?" said Lew.

"Barry explained to his dad that the trauma of dealing with Mother's death, the estate and everything that goes with that—the timing is not right for me. So Mr. Murphy is disappointed because he had hoped to see grandchildren before he dies but we all know that wasn't going to happen anyway, right?" A sheepish grin crossed Blue's face. "But Barry and I have been the dearest of friends since we were little kids and that will never change."

"You two were willing to give up a lot to protect each other," said Osborne. "I don't know many marriages that solid."

"Yes, well, along that line," said Blue, getting up from her chair to stand behind Andy and put both hands on his shoulders, "I'm gifting to Andy a fourth of my trust—five million dollars."

"What!" Andy looked up at her in amazement. "Blue, don't do that. I don't need your money."

"Andy, dear heart, all that's left in Mother's estate is maybe a couple hundred thousand. Not enough for you to retire on, even." Blue sat back in the chair and leaned forwards to grasp both of Andy's hands. "I want you to enjoy life for a change. Travel, go see those fishing tournaments, participate." Blue's face lit up. "I know! Why don't you sponsor your own tournament—become a player, Andy. A real player in that business. You know you'd love it. You know how to do it, too."

"I don't really fish, Blue," said Andy, but he was sitting straighter in his chair. "I work the stats, the fundamentals—not the damn fish. I don't like to fish."

"So? Hire Ray Pradt to be your fishing pro. He can be your consultant. Think of all the fun you can have."

"But, Blue, why— "

"Because you stood there for twenty-five years, Mr. Reece. You stood there, you took the abuse and you were there for me. Now no argument!" She laughed, cuffing him lightly on the cheek.

"And what about you, young lady," said Osborne. "What are your plans for yourself?"

Blue leaned forward to put both hands on Lew's desk and said, "I am going to continue my training as a therapist specializing in drug and alcohol treatment. The money will allow me to build a treatment center for adolescents on our property. My plan is to make it a place where kids—kids like me—can find their way back. That's what I want.

"Fifteen million bucks can make that happen, don't you think?"

THIRTY-TWO

EARLY THE NEXT morning at McDonald's, Jim Craige-meier took center stage with some interesting news. "I was helping Frances with the shop books yesterday when one of the neighbors stopped in," he said. "Seems they caught a young kid who'd swiped his dad's .22-caliber pistol and was shooting squirrels in the neighborhood. He owned up to being the guilty party who killed little Daisy, Mildred's pet.

"Yep," said Jim, "there's a kid who'll be trouble down the road."

"You betcha," said all the old guys in concert, shaking their heads over the steaming mugs of coffee.

FOUR HOURS LATER, Frances was twisting her hands nervously as she waited in the anteroom at St. Mary's Church. The funeral service for Mildred Taggert was scheduled to begin in half an hour. A few people had arrived and taken their places in the pews near the front of the altar. Waiting with Frances and Father Votruba were Osborne, Ray and Lew. Gina had had to leave early that morning for meetings in Madison—the state authorities were anxious to hear how the hunting and fishing license information had been compromised.

"Oh, I don't expect many people to come, really," said Frances. Her smile was as crooked as ever and tension was obvious in her eyes. Osborne couldn't blame her. Over the past few days she had had to make the arrangements for her sister to be buried on the reservation, work with a probate lawyer so she could reopen Mildred's Food Shop, and get her literature paper in on time. She had insisted on completing the latter even though Osborne had called the school on her behalf and everyone there was quite willing to give her an extension.

"Mildred wasn't the warmest person, I know," said Frances, continuing to prepare herself for a very low turnout. "She scared little kids." But even as Frances made the excuses, there was a warmth in her eyes and Osborne recognized the affection she had had for the crotchety old woman who had done the best she could to give two young girls a better start in life.

"She taught you how to be a businesswoman," said Lew. "Think about that. You know how to manage inventory, bookkeeping and how a small grocery has to be run. You know the retail business. Not many girls your age are so experienced."

"Yes," said Frances, brightening, "she didn't have to do that either." She reached into her purse, then hesitated. "Dr. Osborne, I'm wondering—would you look at this quote I want to read for Mrs. Taggert?" She held out an index card with handwriting scrawled across it. "I'm not sure if it's the right thing to say. It's from Emily Dickenson—we've been studying her poetry in my lit class."

Osborne took the card from her hand and read the quote: "The last night that she lived, it was a common night, except the dying: this to us made nature different."

"Mildred would approve," said Osborne, handing it back to her. "Blunt. To the point. And wasn't that what Mildred was all about?"

FIFTEEN MINUTES BEFORE the funeral Mass was to begin, the church was half full. Frances peered through the curtains in the anteroom. "Oh-h-h, my gosh—look how many are here," she said. "Do you think they'll have enough lunch for all these people?"

As the casket moved down the aisle, Osborne was pleased to note that St. Mary's was almost packed. Only a few pews at the very back remained empty. The crowd was quite a mix: youngsters with parents, men and women in business suits, truck drivers, maintenance workers, the entire staff from the insurance office down the street from the shop, elderly folk. Every Loon Lake resident who had ever needed a box of diapers, peanut butter, dish soap, cigarettes or a late night snack when all other stores were closed seemed to be there.

"Oh," Frances was breathless as she started the walk down the aisle behind the casket, "Mildred would be pleased."

She looked up at Osborne who said, "Yep, she might have even cracked a smile."

THE MASS AND THE memorials that followed were the talk of Loon Lake for the next week. To Frances's great surprise, four people walked up to the podium to share their memories of fierce Mildred.

First, the Mayor spoke of her contribution to the community; then, a middle-aged man said he owed his happy marriage to Mildred as she sold paper valentines when he was a kid, making it possible for him to buy one for the little girl who was now his wife. A young mother said her children learned to make change buying their penny candy from Mildred, and then there was the cook from the Loon Lake Café who knew where he could always get an extra dozen eggs at five a.m.

The Mass and memorial service ended with Father Votruba inviting everyone for lunch next door in the school cafeteria.

LUNCH AFTER A funeral at St. Mary's, prepared by the ladies of the church, was a ritual that Osborne always enjoyed. It was a time to catch up with former patients and old friends as everyone piled their plates with fried chicken then sat down at the low tables built for children.

Frances appeared more relaxed as she set her plate down between Ray and Osborne. Ray, carrying a large box in his arms, had arrived a little late to the cafeteria.

"What's he up to?" said Lew, nudging Osborne with her elbow.

"Don't ask me," said Osborne.

"Frances," said Ray, "I understand that Mildred wished to be cremated, is that correct?"

"Yes," said Frances, hesitant. "I'm sorry about that."

"Sorry—why?" said Ray. "Oh, I know, you think I need the money for digging the grave?"

Frances nodded.

"Not to worry, Frances. We don't dig graves this time of the year anyway."

"Ah, Ray—" Lew waved a cautionary finger at him and Osborne knew exactly what she was thinking: no need for Ray to describe what happens to those poor souls who have to wait for a spring thaw before they are laid to rest. He had been known to embellish the details.

But Ray had something else in mind. He reached down for the box he'd carried in, set it on his chair and opened the top flaps. Getting to his feet, he paused, standing straight with his arms crossed until he had the attention of everyone in the cafeteria.

"Folks...Frances...I felt that we should have something very special for Mrs. Mildred Taggert. So I...personally...commissioned an urn that will be... most appropriate for our late friend." He reached into the box and pulled out a dark brown shape that was over a foot tall and about eight inches wide. He held it high in each direction so everyone could see.

"This is a model of an all-brass raccoon that will be finished shortly for Frances to use to contain Mildred's ashes. Now...hold on to your potatoes, everyone... I'll set it over here for all to see." He walked over to place it on the table near the guest book. "Frances, you choose where you would like to keep the urn but I was thinking it might go up on the shelf with the rest of Mildred's collection. It's up to you."

Frances walked over to Ray and took the raccoon from his hands. She smiled at him and at all the people in the cafeteria. "Thank you, Ray," she said. "Thank you, everyone for coming today. Just so you know, I've been told the shop can reopen next week. And, as you can see, thanks to Ray Pradt—Mildred will be there, too."

As she sat down to finish her lunch, Frances smiled her crooked smile at Osborne and Lew. A smile crooked all right—but happy.

THIRTY-THREE

THAT EVENING OSBORNE and Lew nestled beside each other in front of the fireplace at his house. She was taking Thursday off and he had persuaded her, without much difficulty, to let him cook that evening. It was a meal he could not damage: filet mignon medium rare, baked potato with sour cream and his specialty— Brussels sprouts with toasted almonds.

"Move closer," he said, pulling her towards him. She had changed into the flannel pajamas that he gave her for her birthday. White with a blue pattern, she looked soft, even fragile as her face glowed in the light from the fireplace.

"Funny thing," said Osborne as he put an arm around her shoulders, "for such an ugly event—and by that I mean Nolan Reece's death—the difference it will make in the lives of more than a few people is not bad."

"No," said Lew, "it isn't. And you're right—that is ironic. I would like to have known that woman if only to understand her better."

"That reminds me of Ray's comment—it would have been nice to hear Jake Cahak's side of the story."

"Well, life never gives you all the answers, does it? Speaking of Jake, as I left the office today I had an e-mail from Gina. They've located the computer that he was sending the credit card data to—it's in a coffee house in Montreal. Looks like the connection knew something was up when they didn't hear from him in some sort of code they had. All parties have disappeared. The place is under surveillance but they're ninety-nine percent sure they're dealing with a very savvy Russian operation."

"Hmm, can't say Jake wasn't willing to take a risk dealing with people like that."

"No—though I wonder if he got the big picture."

"I'm willing to take a risk or two, Lewellyn."

"Really," she grinned at him, "like riding horseback in panty hose?"

"No panty hose."

She laughed and laughed, then said, "I have new information—long underwear also works."

"But it's summer—it'll be ninety degrees. Long underwear? I have a better idea."

"Which is?"

"A Jeep. We only fish in places you can get to with four-wheel drive."

"Oh. Okay. So what's this risk you want to take?"

"I love you."

She was quiet. "Not sure I can match that."

"Not sure or don't want to?"

"Just…give me time."

IT WAS MIDNIGHT when they turned away from each other. He gazed out the window beside his bed. The snow sparkled. He would remember this night. Those breasts. That moon.